"If you were a really good neighbor, you'd offer to sleep with me."

Breanna stared at him, certain she'd misunderstood what he'd just said. "Excuse me?"

Adam grinned. "You know, so you could wake me up every hour and look at the pupils of my eyes. Isn't that what you're supposed to do with somebody who might have a concussion? What else did you think I meant?" His eyes held a knowing twinkle.

"I knew what you meant," she replied, wondering if her cheeks appeared as red as they felt. "But if you're that concerned about it, I highly recommend an emergency room at one of the local hospitals."

"I like my idea better." The twinkle in his eyes faded and his smile fell. "Breanna." He reached out and touched her cheek with his warm fingertips. "I'm right next door if anything happens or if you just get afraid. I can be over here in seconds."

Dear Reader,

The days are hot and the reading is hotter here at Silhouette Intimate Moments. Linda Turner is back with the next of THOSE MARRYING McBRIDES! in *Always a McBride*. Taylor Bishop has only just found out about his familial connection—and he has no idea it's going to lead him straight to love.

In *Shooting Starr*, Kathleen Creighton ratchets up both the suspense and the romance in a story of torn loyalties you'll long remember. Carla Cassidy returns to CHEROKEE CORNERS in *Last Seen...*, a novel about two people whose circumstances ought to prevent them from falling in love but don't. *On Dean's Watch* is the latest from reader favorite Linda Winstead Jones, and it will keep you turning the pages as her federal marshal hero falls hard for the woman he's supposed to be keeping an undercover watch over. *Roses After Midnight*, by Linda Randall Wisdom, is a suspenseful look at the hunt for a serial rapist—and the blossoming of an unexpected romance. Finally, take a look at Debra Cowan's *Burning Love* and watch passion flare to life between a female arson investigator and the handsome cop who may be her prime suspect.

Enjoy them all—and come back next month for more of the best and most exciting romance reading around.

Yours,

Leslie J. Wainger
Executive Editor

Please address questions and book requests to:
Silhouette Reader Service
U.S.: 3010 Walden Ave., P.O. Box 1325, Buffalo, NY 14269
Canadian: P.O. Box 609, Fort Erie, Ont. L2A 5X3

Last Seen...

CARLA CASSIDY

INTIMATE MOMENTS™

Published by Silhouette Books

America's Publisher of Contemporary Romance

SILHOUETTE BOOKS

ISBN 0-373-27303-7

LAST SEEN...

Copyright © 2003 by Carla Bracale

Visit Silhouette at www.eHarlequin.com

Printed in U.S.A.

Books by Carla Cassidy

CARLA CASSIDY

is an award-winning author who has written over fifty books for Silhouette. In 1995, she won Best Silhouette Romance from *Romantic Times* for *Anything for Danny*. In 1998, she also won a Career Achievement Award for Best Innovative Series from *Romantic Times*.

Carla believes the only thing better than curling up with a good book to read is sitting down at the computer with a good story to write. She's looking forward to writing many more books and bringing hours of pleasure to readers.

Chapter 1

"I always did have a thing for Pocahontas." The middle-aged man with the paunchy waistline grinned, exposing two missing teeth on the upper right side of his mouth.

Breanna James stifled a groan and instead toyed with the end of her braid and smiled coyly. "Then I guess this is your lucky night, cowboy," she replied. She'd be teased unmercifully by her fellow vice cops over the Pocahontas reference but she couldn't worry about that now.

"So...what are you doing out here in the middle of the night?" she asked the man.

"Looking for a party, sweet thing," he replied.

"What kind of a party?"

He grinned eagerly. "I was thinking maybe I could give you twenty-five bucks."

"Sounds like my kind of party," she replied and

released her hold on her long braid. "And what would I have to do for that twenty-five dollars?"

He named a specific sex act and Breanna nodded. "You've got a deal, cowboy," she replied. "How about we go back here in the alley." She pointed to the dark alleyway between two storefronts where she knew two fellow officers were waiting to make the arrest.

He started into the alley, but stopped when he realized she wasn't following him. He slapped his forehead in a comical gesture of absentmindedness, then dug a twenty and five ones from his pocket and handed them to her.

"Now we're ready to party," she said as she tucked the bills into the purse she carried.

Eagerly, he walked into the alley, Breanna just behind him. "Hey, cowboy, you said you've always had a thing for Pocahontas. You ever had a fantasy about a woman cop?"

He stopped walking and frowned thoughtfully. "No, but now that you mention it, it might be kind of fun with handcuffs and all."

The man shouldn't be arrested for solicitation, Breanna thought. He should be arrested for stupidity. It wasn't until the two male officers stepped out of the shadows that he realized he was busted.

His smile fell and he cursed soundly, but didn't fight the officers as they handcuffed him and led him to an unmarked car along the curb.

"That's it for tonight." Abe Solomon, Breanna's partner, grinned. "You did good, Pocahontas. Looks like John, one Mr. Craig Bullock, won't be looking for a date again anytime soon."

She smiled at the gray-haired Abe. "All I know is

I can't wait to get out of this outfit and into a baggy T-shirt and I hope I never see a pair of spike heels again in my life.''

Abe chuckled. "Ah, but you wear them so well."

"Thank goodness I won't have to put them on for at least another week." Saturday nights Breanna often worked as an undercover prostitute, a detail she abhorred.

She and Abe got into their car to head back to the Cherokee Corners police station. "So, you have big plans for your days off?"

"Tomorrow my mother has planned one of her family gatherings. You know she's only happy when she has all of us under one roof." Breanna sighed tiredly. "It will be the usual madness and mayhem."

"Count your blessings. Some of us without families would give anything for a little bit of that madness and mayhem."

Breanna's heart instantly went out to her partner. Abe had lost his wife two years ago and they'd never had children. At fifty-five years old, his parents were gone and he'd been an only child.

She placed a hand on his forearm. "Come over to Mom and Dad's tomorrow. You know they'd love to have you join us."

Abe smiled. "Thanks, honey, but I've got a date with a basement that needs cleaning."

Breanna wrinkled her nose. "You know dinner at my parents' house would be far more entertaining than cleaning your basement."

"True, but it would also be far less productive. Besides, I promised myself if I plowed through the basement I'd take off and do a little fishing." He pulled into the parking lot in front of the brick building that housed the police department.

"Well, if you change your mind, the offer stands," Breanna replied. She and Abe had been partners for the past five years and Breanna thought of Abe as a favorite uncle. Every time he spoke of retirement, Breanna got a sick feeling in the pit of her stomach.

Thirty minutes later she walked out of the building, eager to get home, to kiss her sweet little girl and get some much needed sleep.

More than anything she couldn't wait to get out of the tiny leather skirt and midriff blouse, the black lace hose and the dangerously high spiked heels. She looked like a floozy, which, of course, had been the idea. But, after standing out on a street corner for the past four hours being propositioned, she felt dusty and dirty and wanted a long, hot shower.

As always, a sense of homecoming engulfed her as the rambling Victorian two-story house came into view. The rest of the houses on the street were dark. It was after two and most people were asleep, but as usual Rachel had left the front porch light on for Breanna. Thank goodness for Rachel.

She barely gave the tiny cottage on the side of her property a glance as she pulled into the driveway. The place had been empty for months, much to Breanna's landlord's chagrin.

She shut off her car and climbed out. She had only taken a couple of steps toward the house when she froze, an uneasy tickling sensation at the back of her neck. As a cop, she never ignored this nebulous feeling.

She opened her purse and placed her hand on the butt of the gun resting inside as she looked around.

Nothing seemed amiss at the front of the house. There was nobody lurking in the shadows, no reason for her to feel what she felt.

Then she heard it...the almost imperceptible slap of a bare foot against the grass. She shifted her gaze sideways and that's when she saw him...coming toward her from out of the shadows in front of the cottage.

Without hesitation, she pulled the gun from her purse and fell into an official stance, legs apart, gun held steadily before her with both hands.

"Whoa!" The deep voice broke the silence of the night and he instantly raised his hands out from his sides. "I hope you don't intend to shoot first and ask questions later."

Shadows still clung to him, making it impossible for her to discern his facial features, but she could see the broad width of his shoulders, his slim hips and long legs. "Who are you and what are you doing out here?" she asked as she kept the gun focused on the center of his body.

"Can I lower my arms without getting shot?" he asked.

"Not until you answer my questions."

"My name is Adam Spencer. I moved into the cottage this evening and I was just sitting on the porch relaxing before going to bed."

"Awfully late to be relaxing on a porch. Who did you rent the place from?"

"His name is Herman DeMoser. He looks like a young Jerry Lewis with Jimmy Durante's nose."

Breanna had never thought about it before, but the description perfectly fit her landlord, Herman. She eyed the stranger for another long moment. "You can put your arms down,'' she said, but didn't lower her gun.

''I had visions of a welcome wagon greeting me to the neighborhood,'' he said wryly. ''None of my visions involved a beautiful woman holding me at gunpoint.''

Suddenly Breanna felt a little silly, aware that she might have overreacted because of her police training. She finally lowered the gun, although she didn't put it back in her purse. ''I apologize. All I saw was a man coming toward me from the shadows and...well...a woman can't be too careful.''

''No, I apologize. I should have realized how it would look coming at you in the dark at this time of night.'' The shadows that had hidden his features fell away as he stepped closer, into the faint illumination of her porch light.

Her breath caught in her chest at the sight of his handsome features. Intense blue eyes gazed at her with obvious interest. His dark brown hair had just enough curl to fall impishly over his broad forehead. He had a classic nose over nicely shaped, sensual lips. A small cleft in his chin only added to his attractiveness.

As she watched, his gaze slid down the length of her, lingering on her bare midriff, then moved slowly down her lace-covered legs. She felt that gaze deep in the pit of her stomach, like a heated caress over her skin.

It had been a very long time since the sight of a handsome man had caused her heart to beat just a little bit faster, her hands to feel slightly clammy and shaky. She was obviously overtired and her reaction to him made her more than a little bit irritable.

"It was nice meeting you, but it's late and I've had a long night. I would highly recommend in the future you don't sneak up on a woman alone in the middle of the night."

He nodded. "Point taken. Good night." He stepped back into the shadows, then turned and walked toward the cottage. A moment later she heard the front door of the small house open, then close.

Only then did she tuck her gun back into her purse and head for her own front door. As she stepped into the hallway, she kicked off her high-heeled shoes and allowed her toes to splay in the throw rug that covered the gleaming hardwood floor.

When she'd first viewed the house for the possibility of renting, it had been a mess. Abused by former tenants, neglected over the course of time, the Victorian beauty seemed destined to remain abandoned for the rest of its days.

Breanna had seen the potential and had come to an agreement with Herman. For the next three years she would pay a minimal rental fee a month and she would do all the repair work at her own expense.

Since she had moved in, the house had slowly transformed itself thanks to the labor of her family. Her elder brother, Clay, had helped sand and refinish the floors. Her older sister, Savannah, and her mother had wallpapered and painted and Breanna's father had rebuilt the front porch and seen to the painting of the outside of the house.

Even though she'd only been in the house two years, the place had quickly become home and she now couldn't imagine living any place else.

As she walked through the living room, she was

surprised to see the kitchen light on and hear the faint sound of a television playing.

Rachel Davies, Breanna's live-in nanny, sat at the kitchen table, staring at the small portable television on the counter.

"Can't sleep?"

Rachel jumped in surprise and whirled around to face Breanna. "You scared me," she exclaimed.

Breanna smiled apologetically. "I just assumed you heard me come in." She sat in the chair opposite Rachel. "Nervous about tomorrow?"

Rachel smiled and tucked a strand of her long blond hair behind her ear. "More than I thought," she admitted.

The next day Rachel was going on her first date in almost two years. "It's just a picnic, Rachel, and David is a very nice man."

"I know…but I can't help but remember that I thought Michael was a nice man."

Breanna reached across the table and covered her friend's hand with her own. "That's in your past, and now it's time for you to look forward to a great future filled with love and respect."

Rachel squeezed her hand. "I don't know what I would have done without you."

Breanna pulled her hand back and laughed. "You seem to have it backward. I can't imagine what I would do without you! And speaking of that, how was my little munchkin today?"

Rachel smiled. "Wonderful, as usual. I swear, Breanna, Maggie is the brightest, sweetest child I've ever known."

Pride swelled up inside Breanna. "And you are obviously a woman of enormous judgement, which is why I hired you to take care of her in the first place.''

"By the way, we have a new neighbor in the cottage. I watched him unloading this evening and he's a definite hunk!''

"I know. I met him.''

Rachel frowned. "You did? When?''

"Just a few minutes ago when I pulled my gun on him.'' Breanna tried not to think about that swirl of heat that had swept over her as Adam Spencer had looked at her.

"You pulled your gun on him?'' Rachel asked in surprise.

"He came out of the darkness at me without warning. I didn't know who he was or what he wanted.''

"And what did he want?''

Breanna shrugged. "I guess just to introduce himself to me.''

Rachel smiled wickedly. "I'd like to hold him at gunpoint and have my way with him.''

Breanna laughed. "This from a woman who is too nervous to sleep because she has a date with a preacher tomorrow.''

"You know what they say about the preacher's kids…they're the wildest ones in town.''

Breanna smiled. "Not in this case. David Mandell is a nice guy.'' She stood, suddenly exhausted and more than a little eager to kiss her sweet sleeping daughter on her cheek. "I'm off to bed and if you're wise, you'll do the same. You don't want to scare David tomorrow with huge black bags under your eyes.''

Rachel nodded. "I'll be up in just a few minutes.''

The two said their good-nights, then Breanna

climbed the wide staircase. She peeked into her daughter's bedroom just to assure herself that all was well, then went directly into her own bedroom and the private bath.

She never kissed her daughter when she had the stink of the streets on her, when her skin crawled from all the men who had whispered dirty things to her, leered at her with hungry eyes.

Minutes later she stepped out of the hot shower, dried off, then pulled on her comfortable cotton nightshirt. It took several minutes to brush and dry her long, thick dark hair, then she quietly crept into Maggie's room.

A cartoon character night-light illuminated the area around the twin bed, and Maggie's little face peeked out from beneath the covers.

Breanna sat in the chair at the edge of the bed and breathed in the scent of the room...the sweet mixture of peach bubble bath and childhood.

She loved to watch her daughter as she slept, loved the way Maggie's little cupid bow lips puffed out with each breath, the way her curly brown hair decorated the pillow.

Kurt Randolf had been a bad choice for a boyfriend, a worse choice for a husband, but his genes and Breanna's had combined to create the miracle Breanna had named Maggie.

When she was awake, she was a bundle of energy and curiosity, a delight that made all the heartache of Kurt worthwhile.

Breanna stood, leaned over and kissed Maggie's sweet cheek, then left the bedroom and headed for her own room across the hall. She turned out her light and used the illumination of the moonlight streaking in through the window to guide her into bed.

She had just pulled the sheet up and snuggled in when the phone rang. She quickly snatched up the receiver on her nightstand, dread coursing through her. Good news rarely came at this hour of the night.

"Hello?"

Silence.

"Hello?" she repeated, then a soft click greeted her. The line filled with a woman's voice singing the standard lullaby of "Rock-A-Bye Baby."

Breanna knew instantly it was some sort of a recording and so she remained silent, listening to the soft melodic voice.

When the last note faded away she heard a second click. The line remained open and she knew somebody was there because she could hear breathing.

"Who is this?" She sat up in bed. "What do you want? You must have a wrong number."

A noise answered her. She wasn't sure but it sounded like a male sob, then the line went dead.

She held the receiver for a long moment, fighting the sense of unease that crept through her. Just a wrong number, she told herself as she finally hung up the phone.

Rather than settling back in her bed, she got up and padded across the hall. Standing in the doorway, she peered in to see Maggie still sleeping peacefully.

There was absolutely no reason for Breanna to feel such a strong sense of disquiet, but she did. She returned to her bedroom and once again slid beneath the sheet. A wrong number…or somebody's idea of a prank, she told herself again.

Still, it was a very long time before she finally drifted off to sleep.

* * *

Adam Spencer sat on the shabby sofa that was part of the furnishings in the small cottage right next to Breanna James's residence. Finding this place for rent so close to his quarry had been a godsend. Although the ramshackle cottage wouldn't have been his first choice of a temporary residence, it would do for now.

"Damn you, Kurt," he said aloud as he popped the top off a bottle of beer. He was tired…exhausted in fact. He'd driven from Kansas City, Missouri, to the town of Cherokee Corners, Oklahoma, that day and had spent most of the evening unloading the personal items he'd brought with him. He should be in bed, but he knew sleep would be elusive.

He needed to process his initial impression of Breanna James. That she was strikingly beautiful didn't surprise him. Kurt had always dated beautiful women.

He frowned and took a sip of the cold beer as he thought of his cousin. Kurt had been an adventurer, both in his relationships and with the way he lived his life. As the only son of wealthy parents he'd enjoyed too much money and not enough goals.

He'd been buried a week ago after a tragic motorcycle accident. He'd been riding too fast without a helmet on a rain-drenched highway. The accident had pretty well summed up Kurt's life…flying too fast with too little sense.

Kurt had clung to life for six long hours in the hospital…long enough to confess to Adam that six years before he'd briefly been married to a woman in Cherokee Corners named Breanna James.

He'd further astonished Adam with the news that there had been a child…a daughter. With his dying breath he'd begged Adam to find them and make sure they were doing okay. Caught up in the emotional turmoil of losing the man who had been like a brother to him, Adam had agreed.

So here he sat in a rental shack next to the woman who had briefly been Kurt's wife. He had yet to see the child, didn't even know her name. But she was the real reason he was here.

Adam had seen his aunt and uncle's utter grief over losing their only son. Kurt's death had devastated them. A grandchild would be a gift, a legacy of the son they had lost.

But Adam didn't intend to tell them of the child's existence until he'd assessed the whole situation. He loved his aunt and uncle, who had raised him since the age of eleven when his own parents had died in a freak small plane accident. He would not invite more pain into the lives of the couple who had raised him.

Kurt's women had always been beautiful, but they'd also always been extremely dysfunctional. Some of them, aware of Kurt's family money, had been nothing more than gold diggers, others had been mentally unbalanced, or on drugs, or just plain needy.

Adam sighed and took another sip of beer, his thoughts returning to Breanna. It had instantly been obvious she was of Native American descent. High cheekbones gave her face a proud strength, but her long-lashed, liquid brown eyes had hinted at vulnerability.

Her long black hair had been tightly confined in a braid and he'd found himself wondering what she'd look like with those rich, thick strands loose and flowing around her shoulders.

Her skimpy clothing had done little to hide a lean, sweet, killer of a body. He frowned and downed the last of his beer.

"Damn you, Kurt," he repeated. He'd spent most of his life cleaning up Kurt's messes and he had a feeling that this was going to be the monster of messes.

He intended to hang around here for a week or two and see exactly what kind of a woman Breanna James was before he told his uncle Edward and aunt Anita that they had a grandchild.

His biggest fear at the moment was that somehow, someway he was going to have to figure out a way to tell them that the mother of their grandchild was a prostitute.

Chapter 2

It was just after ten when Breanna heard a car door slam shut and her mother's voice drifting in through the open living-room window. She went to the window and moved aside the gauzy curtain to see her mother talking to Adam Spencer.

Rita Birdsong James was a short, petite woman who had never met a stranger in her life. Breanna groaned inwardly as she wondered what sort of personal information Rita was giving to her new neighbor.

When Breanna had gotten out of bed at eight, Adam Spencer had already been up and weeding the pathetically neglected flower bed in his front yard.

Breanna had spent far too long standing at her bedroom window watching him. She told herself she was observing him as a cop would any person who invaded her personal space. But it was a woman's gaze that admired the play of his arm and back muscles as he worked. It was a woman's gaze that noted how the bright sunshine teased hints of impish red into his dark brown hair.

She had whirled away from the window, irritated with herself and the stir of heat her observations had created in the pit of her stomach.

She now returned to the kitchen table and the cup of coffee she'd been enjoying, knowing her mother would come inside when she was finished chatting up Adam.

Ten minutes later, Rita flew into the kitchen, dark eyes snapping and a satisfied smile on her face. At fifty-eight years old, Rita was still a stunningly beautiful woman. Her face was smooth, unlined…as if life hadn't touched it with heartache or strife.

Her short hair was just as black as it had ever been, the cut emphasizing her defined cheekbones and generous smile. She was like a china doll in a collector's case, always perfectly made-up and elegantly dressed.

"So did you spill all the James's deep, dark family secrets?" Breanna asked.

Rita laughed and walked to the cabinet to grab a coffee cup. "I wish we had some deep, dark family secrets to spill. It would keep life interesting." She poured herself a cup of coffee, then joined Breanna at the table. "And where's my baby girl this beautiful morning?"

"With Rachel. They went to the grocery store. Rachel decided she needed a few more things for her picnic lunch this afternoon."

"It's nice to see her opening up to the idea of dating again." She raised a dark, perfectly formed brow and peered at Breanna over the rim of her coffee cup.

"That's something you might consider. He's very handsome and he's not married."

"Don't even start," Breanna warned.

"He's a painter, studying Native American art. I told him all about the Cherokee Cultural Center and invited him to dinner this afternoon."

Breanna wanted to protest. She'd been looking forward to their first barbecue of the year, to a relaxing time with family and close friends. But she knew it did no good to protest. As her father, Thomas, often said, the Birdsongs were the most stubborn people in the Cherokee nation.

The sound of the front door opening halted any further conversation. "Grandma!" Maggie exclaimed as she burst into the kitchen.

"Hello, my little doe. Come give me my kiss." Rita opened her arms and Maggie climbed up on her lap.

"Look what Rachel got for me." Maggie held out a pink cord necklace; dangling from it was a plastic charm in the shape of a horse.

"She's named him Thunder and swears she's never taking him off," Rachel said as she entered the kitchen carrying a sack of groceries.

"Never taking him off?" Breanna smiled indulgently at her daughter.

"Not even to take a bath," Maggie replied. She wiggled down from Rita's lap, unable to remain confined for another moment. "I've got to show him to Mr. Bear. Mr. Bear always wanted a horse friend." With these words Maggie tore out of the kitchen, her footsteps resounding as she raced up the stairs to her bedroom.

"Ah, to have her energy," Rita exclaimed.

"Mother, you have more energy than ten Maggies put together," Breanna replied dryly.

"Your father says there are times it's quite irritating. Did I tell you I was mad at him?"

As Rita began to catalog her most recent complaints against her husband, Breanna thought of her parents' marriage.

For thirty-eight years they had shared a spirited relationship. They fought as loud and passionately as they loved...and it was obvious to anyone who spent any time in their company that they were true soul mates.

That's what Breanna had once wished for herself. The kind of love that strengthened rather than diminished with time, the kind of commitment that didn't have to be spoken aloud but was just there...in the heart...in the soul.

Her brief, disastrous marriage to Kurt had destroyed those dreams and broken her heart. Despite her mother's wish to the contrary, she had no desire to date, no desire to involve a man in her life. She and Maggie were just fine alone.

"Well, I'd better get out of here," Rita said. She stood and finished the last of her coffee. "We're having everyone's favorite food today," she said as Breanna walked her to the front door. "I'm putting beef ribs on the grill for your father and Clay. I'm making bean bread for Savannah and grape dumplings for you."

"Sounds wonderful. What can I bring?" Breanna asked as they stepped out on her front porch.

"Your new neighbor. I told him you'd pick him up at three."

"Mother!" Breanna protested.

Rita reached up and kissed her youngest daughter on the cheek. "He's a stranger in a strange town and the Cherokee are known for their hospitality. I expect you to honor your heritage and be a gracious hostess. And I know you will."

After the two had said their goodbyes, Breanna watched her mother get into her car, then she went back into the kitchen where Rachel was putting together her picnic lunch.

She grinned at Breanna. "So, it sounds like I'm not the only one who has a date this afternoon."

"This is definitely not a date," Breanna protested and poured herself a fresh cup of coffee. "I'm merely transporting a person to my parents' home for a barbecue."

"I think your mother hopes it will be something quite different," Rachel observed as she slathered bread with mustard.

Breanna sat back down at the table and sighed. "I'm afraid my sister and brother and I have disappointed Mother when it comes to our love lives."

"I'm surprised Clay has never married," Rachel said.

Breanna shook her head as she thought of her older brother. "Clay has never had a lasting relationship with anyone. He spends all his time either at a crime scene or cooped up in his lab."

"A terrible waste of hunk-hood," Rachel exclaimed.

Breanna grinned. She knew her brother was considered a hunk by most of the women in Cherokee Corners, but he was positively possessed by his work as a crime scene technician.

"It's so sad that Savannah and her husband seemed

to have such a wonderful marriage and then he got killed in that car accident last year.'' Rachel grabbed the sliced ham from the refrigerator and continued. ''And it isn't your fault that Kurt turned out to be a selfish little boy who wasn't prepared to take on the role of husband and father.''

''Sometimes it feels like my fault,'' Breanna replied. ''I should have seen the signs, I shouldn't have married him so soon after meeting him.''

''And I should have seen the signs that Michael was a possessive, obsessive, brutal man, but I didn't until it was too late.'' Rachel touched her cheek, where a small scar puckered the skin. ''I had no idea what he was capable of.''

''At least he's behind bars where he belongs,'' Breanna said. ''Unfortunately they don't put immature men in jail.''

Rachel grinned. ''If they did, they'd definitely need to build more jails.''

''Isn't that the truth,'' Breanna agreed.

Later that afternoon, as Breanna dressed for the family barbecue, she thought about her brother and sister and how sad it was that none of the James siblings had been successful in their quest for happy marriages.

Savannah had come the closest, having been married to <u>Jimmy Tallfeather</u> for just a little over a year before tragedy had ended their marriage. The entire family had been worried about her because she still clung to her grief as jealously, as deeply as she had on the day she'd learned her husband had been stolen from her.

Maybe Adam Spencer was the man to bring Savannah back to life. Maybe that had been her mother's ultimate hope. This thought made Breanna less tense about spending any time at all in the handsome newcomer's company.

She would suffer the short drive from her own home to her parents', then introduce him to Savannah and hope for an instant love connection between the two.

At exactly quarter to three, Adam stepped out on his front porch and looked at the house next door. She was a cop, not a prostitute and the knowledge filled Adam with relief. When he'd met Breanna's mother that morning, one of the first things she'd shared with him was the fact that her family was comprised of law enforcement officials.

It would certainly be easier to tell Uncle Edward and Aunt Anita that the mother of their grandchild was a vice cop rather than a prostitute.

He was interested in learning more about the James family, who would forever be bound to him by the existence of a little girl. He wanted to see that Breanna and her daughter were okay, set up a trust fund for Kurt's daughter, then go on with his own life knowing he had cleaned up Kurt's final mess.

He sat down on the porch stoop, wondering if she would be one of those women who were perpetually late for everything. He looked down the street, breathing in the sweet scent of spring that filled the air.

Cherokee Corners had been a surprise. He'd expected a dusty little town and instead had discovered a bustling metropolis. The downtown area was built on a square, with the city buildings in the center, and unique shops and familiar chain stores surrounding them.

He'd found Breanna's home on the west side of town, only a few miles from the Cherokee Cultural Center that included a replica of a village and Cherokee life a hundred years before.

Rita Birdsong James had indicated that she spent a lot of time at the center and was actively involved in the running of the educational tourist attraction.

And he'd told her he was an artist...a painter, for crying out loud. He swiped a hand through his curly hair and sighed. He'd regretted the words the minute they had left his lips, but she'd surprised him by asking what had brought him to Cherokee Corners and what he did for a living.

Painting had sprung into his head because he'd found a half-completed paint-by-number of a Native American on horseback in the kitchen when he'd moved in. Telling Rita Birdsong James that he was an artist leaped to his lips before he'd had an opportunity to think it through.

Of course, an artist was certainly more exciting, more exotic than his real job as the owner of a small, but successful accounting firm. And he had a feeling that telling Rita that he was interested in Cherokee culture had granted him instant access to their family gathering that afternoon.

At that moment Breanna's front door opened and a little girl danced outside, followed by Breanna. Adam stood and his heart jumped into his throat as his gaze was captured by the child.

Kurt. Her long, curly brown hair was all Kurt's, as was the slender oval of her facial structure. As she smiled up at her mother, another arrow pierced through Adam as he saw the dimple that danced in one cheek…just like the dimple that had made Kurt's smile so infectious.

Breanna saw him and waved him over as she opened the driver door to her car. "Good afternoon," she said as he approached. "This is my daughter, Maggie. Maggie, this is Mr. Spencer. He's going with us to Grandma's house."

"Hi, Maggie." Adam fought the impulse to lean down and grab the child to his chest. He hadn't expected the emotions that now rolled around inside him as he continued to gaze at Kurt's child. "Mr. Spencer is kind of a mouthful. You can call me Adam."

"Okay," Maggie agreed with a bright smile. Even her eyes were all Kurt's…dark gray and sparking with life. "You want to see my horse?" She held out a necklace, where a plastic charm in the shape of a horse dangled. "His name is Thunder."

"That's a fine name for a horse," Adam replied.

"Maggie, get inside and buckle up. We need to hit the road."

As Adam got into the passenger seat, Breanna watched as her daughter buckled into the back seat, then she got in behind the steering wheel.

The shock of seeing Maggie wore off somewhat and he became conscious of Breanna's scent…a mixture of wildflowers and patchouli, slightly exotic and definitely appealing.

Her appearance was just as appealing. Her coral-colored T-shirt was a perfect foil for the darkness of her hair and her white shorts set off the rich, bronze tones of long, shapely legs.

Last night her features had been almost garish with

heavy makeup. Today her face had a freshly scrubbed kind of beauty.

"Tell the truth, Adam." Kurt's voice filled his head. "You've always been jealous of my life and you've always wanted my women." Adam frowned and consciously shoved his cousin's voice out of his head.

"Thank you for letting me ride with you," he said, trying not to dwell on the fact that today her hair was down, loose and flowing and more beautiful than he'd imagined. "It was so nice of your mother to invite me."

She flashed him a quick smile as she backed out of the driveway. "If my mother had her way, all of Cherokee Corners would come to their barbecues. She loves people."

"That was obvious in the brief time I spoke with her."

"She tells me you're a painter. Would I have seen any of your work anywhere?"

Again Adam regretted his impulsive claim. "Only if you rummage through trash cans on a regular basis," he replied dryly. She laughed and a wave of pleasant heat swept through him at the sound of her melodic amusement.

"If that's the case, I hope you don't paint for a living," she replied.

"No. Actually I'm an accountant by trade. That's how I make my living." It felt good, to be able to give her this much truth.

"So what brings you to Cherokee Corners? This isn't exactly a financial center. Unfortunately this town has far too high a quota of people living in poverty."

"My office is in Kansas City. I'm not here in Cherokee Corners permanently. With tax time behind us for the year, I decided to give myself a little vacation and with my interest in Cherokee culture and art, this seemed like the place to spend a month or two."

"Do you have any little girls or boys?" Maggie asked him from the back seat.

Adam turned and again felt that jarring burst of emotion as he looked at her. He tried to steel himself against it. The last thing he wanted was to become emotionally involved with this child and her beautiful mother. "No, honey. I'm afraid I don't. I don't have a wife or children."

"How come?" Maggie asked, her gray eyes gazing at him with open curiosity.

"That's a personal question, Maggie." Her mother replied before Adam got a chance to answer. "It isn't nice to ask personal questions."

"Oh. Is it personal to ask if he could get some kids so I'd have somebody to play with?" Maggie asked.

Breanna flashed Adam an apologetic look. "There aren't any children Maggie's age in the neighborhood and so she's always hoping somebody will move in with kids her age."

"I'm afraid I can't help you, honey," Adam said. "I don't see any kids in my life now or in the future." He turned around to look at Breanna once again. "Your mother mentioned that you all work in law enforcement."

She nodded and made a left turn at an intersection. "My father retired from the police force a year ago. He was chief of police for a number of years. My brother, <u>Clay</u>, works in crime scene investigations, my sister, <u>Savannah, is</u> a homicide cop and I work vice.''

"Rather unusual, isn't it, that all of you chose that line of work?"

She shrugged. "I guess. For me, it was just a natural choice. Dad loved his work and listening to him talk about it as I was growing up, I knew very early that I was going to be a cop, too."

"Why vice?"

"Why not?" she countered. "It's a job somebody needs to do and it's where my superiors feel I'm most needed."

"You had just gotten off work last night when I met you?" he asked. She nodded and he grinned. "You make a very convincing lady of the night."

She cast him a glance that was distinctly cool. "And you almost got yourself shot as a prowler." She returned her focus out the front window.

Prickly, Adam thought. Or maybe it wasn't the best thing to tell a woman she made a perfect streetwalker. Maybe his people skills were rustier than he thought.

He decided the best thing to do was to keep quiet and turned his head to look out the window. They had left the outskirts of Cherokee Corners proper and were passing the Cultural Center and village.

"If you're interested in Cherokee culture, this is the place to spend your time," she said, her voice holding none of the coolness it had moments before.

"That's where my grandma works," Maggie said. "We go there lots of times and do dances and have fun."

"There is something going on there almost every day during the summer months," Breanna explained.

"My mother thinks it's very important to continue to educate people about the Cherokee ways."

"Your father is Cherokee, too?" Adam asked.

Breanna laughed. "No. Dad is one hundred percent fighting Irish, as proud of his heritage as Mother is of hers."

"Must have made interesting supper conversations."

It was obvious speaking about her parents put her at ease. She smiled and nodded. "You don't know the half of it. Both of them are stubborn, passionate people. I should probably warn you. We rarely get through one of these family gatherings without an explosion of fireworks between them, but the fireworks rarely last long."

She pulled down a dirt lane that led to a rambling ranch house. There was not another house in sight in any direction. Cars in a variety of shapes and sizes clogged the circular driveway in front of the house.

She parked the car and turned to Adam. "Do you come from a large family?"

"No. My parents died when I was eleven and I was raised by an aunt and uncle. That is pretty much the extent of my family."

Her dark eyes flashed with a flicker of sympathy. "Oh, I'm sorry."

"Don't be. My aunt and uncle are kind, loving people."

"That's good. But I just wanted to warn you that my family is big and loud and might be quite overwhelming to somebody unaccustomed to big family gatherings."

"Mommy, let's go!" Maggie said plaintively from the back seat.

"Yes, let's go," Breanna agreed and opened her car door. "It looks like most of the gang have already arrived."

It took them only moments to get out of the car and walk down the driveway to the house. Breanna opened the door and they entered a large living room.

Adam's first impression was one of warmth and comfort. It was obvious this room, decorated in earth tones, was the heart of the house. The walls held Native American artwork, all with the common theme of Indians and bears.

"They're all the work of a local artist. Her name is Tamara Greystone. She's a teacher at the high school," Breanna explained. "You might want to look her up...you know, share techniques or whatever."

"I might just do that," he replied, although he had no intention of sharing "techniques" with an artist, who would see through his false claim with ease.

Maggie danced ahead of them and out a sliding glass door. Breanna motioned for Adam to follow her outside.

Nothing Breanna had told him had prepared him for the cacophony of sound coming from the throng of people on the large patio. Breanna had mentioned an older brother and sister, but it was obvious this gathering was bigger than immediate family members only.

He saw Rita James standing with a group of people around the large, brick barbecue. Her gaze caught his and she immediately left the group and approached him and Breanna with a warm smile.

She grabbed his hands in hers. "Adam, I'm so glad you came."

"I appreciate you inviting me," he replied.

She released his hands and smiled at her daughter. "Breanna, why don't you take Adam around and introduce him to everyone."

"All right," she agreed easily.

Over the next few minutes Adam was introduced to enough people that his head spun, trying to remember names and faces. He was introduced to Thomas James, Breanna's father, a tall man with graying red hair and bright blue eyes.

He stood duty over the racks of ribs that sizzled on the barbecue grill. He greeted Adam with a firm handshake and exuded a vigor and energy that belied his age.

Adam was then introduced to Jacob Kincaid, an older man who was Thomas's best friend and the president of the largest bank in Cherokee Corners.

"Jacob is our resident collector," Breanna said. "His house is filled with antiques to die for and he has a wonderful art collection and some of the most exquisite Fabergé eggs you'd ever want to see."

Jacob smiled at Breanna with obvious affection. "I certainly hope Mr. Spencer isn't a cat burglar because if he is, you've just given him a road map to the riches in town."

"Oh, and did I mention his state-of-the-art security system?" Breanna added and both men laughed. After visiting a few minutes with the banker, Breanna excused them and led Adam to a woman seated in a lawn chair. He instantly knew it was Breanna's sister.

The two women looked remarkably alike, except that Savannah's dark, glossy hair was cut short. That, coupled with a profound sadness in her eyes, gave her a look of intense vulnerability. Although she was pleasant, Adam found Breanna far more interesting.

He told himself his only interest was the fact that his life and hers would forever be bound by the child she'd had…Kurt's child.

After they visited with Savannah for a few minutes, Adam was introduced to Breanna's brother, Clay. Clay had brooding good looks, his eyes radiating the intensity of a driven man. Although friendly, he seemed distracted, as if he found his inner thoughts more interesting than those of others.

Breanna introduced him to cousins and aunts and uncles and more friends of the family. It was easy to see that the James family was not only well liked in the town, but also highly respected.

"There's one more person I have to introduce you to," Breanna said, "then it probably won't be long before we eat and you can visit with whomever you please." She led him to another pretty young woman who sat slightly alone on a stone bench surrounded by early blooming spring flowers.

"This is my cousin, Alyssa Whitefeather. Alyssa, this is my new neighbor, Adam Spencer."

Alyssa stood and offered her hand to Adam. "Hello, Mr. Spencer."

Adam took her hand in his and started to return the greeting, but before he could say a word, Alyssa's blue eyes rolled upward and she collapsed in Adam's arms.

Chapter 3

Breanna sat on a chair next to her parents' bed where Alyssa lay pale as a ghost against the dark blue bedspread. Adam had carried her in here, then Breanna had shooed everyone out of the room and closed the door.

She knew the family would return to their activities. Over the years they had all become accustomed to Alyssa's occasional "spells" and knew she would be unconscious for a few minutes, then would awaken and be fine.

What Breanna wanted to know was what had brought on this particular spell? Had it been the touch of Adam's hand? And if that had been it, then what had her cousin "seen"?

She knew there was no point in trying to rouse Alyssa. She'd awaken when she was ready and nothing Breanna did or said would bring her around sooner.

Minutes ticked by, indicated by the tick-tock of the old schoolhouse clock on the wall. It was a sound as familiar as Breanna's mother's heartbeat. Many early mornings, the James's bed had been filled with her parents and the kids, greeting the day with soft talk, giggles and the rhythmic beating of that clock.

Breanna leaned forward as Alyssa released a soft, audible sigh. Her eyes fluttered open and shut...open and shut, then remained open.

"Hi."

Alyssa sat up and looked around as if to orient herself. "Hi."

"Are you okay?" Breanna frowned with concern. Usually when Alyssa came out of one of these spells, she appeared refreshed and alert. This time she appeared fragile and her hand shook as she worried it through a strand of her brown hair.

She hesitated a moment, then nodded. "I'm fine." Once again she swept a strand of her hair behind her ear and frowned. "I haven't done that in quite some time."

"What brought it on? Anything specific? Was it my neighbor?"

Alyssa's frown deepened. "No...I don't think so." Her blue eyes were troubled as she gazed at Breanna. "I felt something dark...something evil from the moment I stepped into the house today." She placed a hand over her heart. "I have a horrible feeling of dread and I don't know what's causing it."

"Have you seen anything?" Breanna asked, referring to the various visions Alyssa had suffered with since she was a small child.

"Blackness. Just blackness." She shivered. "I've never had anything like this before." She swung her legs over the side of the bed and drew a deep breath. "Whenever I've had a vision in the past, it's always been like watching a snippet of a movie in my head. But not this time. This time there was just the blackness and a sense of horror like I've never experienced before."

A slight chill worked up Breanna's spine. "Are you sure you're okay?"

Alyssa drew another deep breath, then offered a tentative smile. "I'm fine, just a little bit embarrassed. I can't imagine what your poor neighbor thinks. You introduce me to him and I faint in his arms."

Breanna offered her a reassuring smile. "Don't worry, I'll tell him you're hypoglycemic and just needed a little sugar boost."

Alyssa leaned across and grabbed Breanna's hand. "Don't look so worried. My feelings and visions don't always mean anything. Stress sometimes triggers an event and things have been really crazy down at the bed-and-breakfast."

Alyssa owned and operated a bed-and-breakfast on the square, along with an ice-cream parlor that was a favorite gathering place.

She stood and released Breanna's hand. "Now, we better get back to the party before we miss all the good food."

Breanna stood as well and opened the door, then stumbled into the solid chest of Adam. Worried blue eyes gazed at her as he grabbed her by the shoulders to steady her. "Is everything all right?" His gaze moved from her to Alyssa, who stood just behind her.

"Everything is fine, Mr. Spencer," Alyssa assured him and he dropped his hands from Breanna's shoulders. "I should apologize. I don't normally faint when introduced to a new person. I'm afraid I haven't been eating right and…'' She allowed her voice to trail off.

''And it's done and over,'' Breanna said firmly. ''Why don't we all rejoin the party. I'm sure they're probably serving up the food now.'' As she moved past Adam in the hallway, she smelled his cologne, a woodsy, masculine scent that stirred something feminine in her.

It irritated her, how this man affected her on some primal level that had nothing to do with intellect and everything to do with sex appeal.

As the three of them walked through the house and out the sliding glass doors to the backyard, she decided she had done her duty and introduced him to everyone. He was now on his own for the remainder of the day.

Sure enough, the food was being served and Breanna left Adam in search of her daughter. She found her sitting on her Aunt Savannah's lap.

''Hey, sweetie. Why don't you go get yourself a plate of food and let me visit with Aunt Savannah for a minute.''

''I'm starving,'' Maggie exclaimed as she jumped down from Savannah's lap. ''Bye, Aunt Savannah, we'll talk more after I eat.''

''It's a deal,'' Savannah replied, the darkness in her eyes momentarily lifted as she smiled at Maggie.

''How are you doing, sis?'' Breanna asked as Maggie scampered away.

''Good,'' Savannah replied, but the sadness in her eyes that had been present for the past year was an indicator to Breanna that the heartache of losing Jimmy still consumed her.

''You look tired. Are you working too many

hours?'' Breanna asked. The entire family had been after Savannah to take some time off, to get away from the misery of seeing murders up close and personal.

Savannah shrugged. ''It's been a long week.

''Still no break in the Maxwell murder?''

''Nothing. Poor man is found naked and dead in front of the public library. Clay has been pulling out his hair because the crime scene was contaminated by dozens of gawkers and we've all been stymied by the fact that Greg Maxwell seemed to be loved by everyone who knew him.''

''Something will break. It always does,'' Breanna said.

''Your new neighbor seems very nice,'' Savannah said.

Breanna looked over to the patio where Adam was talking to her father. The khaki slacks Adam wore hugged his slender hips and long legs and the short-sleeved dress shirt emphasized the width of his chest and the muscles of his biceps. ''I guess. I really don't know him that well. It was Mother who invited him.''

Savannah smiled. ''Big surprise. She's always inviting strays home.''

Breanna looked back over to Adam. He didn't seem like a stray. In her brief acquaintance with him, he appeared to be a man who knew exactly who he was and where he was going. There was a quiet confidence about him she found intriguing, despite the fact that she had no intention of developing any kind of a relationship other than that of good neighbors.

''Come and get a plate,'' Breanna said and pulled her sister to her feet. Breanna fixed herself a plate and joined her daughter at one of the picnic tables that were scattered across the backyard.

"Aunt Savannah said maybe she'll take me to a movie next week," Maggie said.

"That would be nice, wouldn't it?" Breanna replied.

"I like the movies." Maggie grabbed the little horse on her necklace. "I think Thunder would like them, too."

"Mind if I join you?" Adam stood next to the picnic table, his plate in hand.

Breanna wanted to tell him to go sit someplace else, but of course she didn't. "Not at all." She wondered exactly what it was about him that set her so on edge.

He scooted onto the bench next to her, their shoulders bumping as his scent filled her head.

She knew then why he set her on edge, made her uncomfortable and wary. Something about the way he affected her reminded her of those first few weeks with Kurt. Adam Spencer made her feel that same rush of heat, a lick of lust that she'd never felt before Kurt...or since...until now.

Kurt had been a disastrous mistake and so it was only natural that a man who stirred the same kind of feelings would evoke a defensive wariness in her.

"You have a wonderful family," he said.

"They are very special," Breanna replied. "I'm not sure what I would have done without them in the past five years. Being a single parent isn't easy."

"I imagine not." He frowned and focused on his food.

"What about you? Do you eventually want a wife and children?" She assumed he was in his late twenties or early thirties. Didn't most men of that age start to think about creating families?

"Not me," he said firmly. "I much prefer to be footloose and fancy-free."

"Your foot is loose?" Maggie eyed him with a touch of childish horror. "Does it hurt?"

"No, honey, my foot isn't really loose. That's just an expression." Adam smiled at Maggie. "My feet work just fine."

"Rabbits' feet are good," Maggie said after a moment of thought. "And frogs' feet. They help jump...jump...jump."

As Adam and Maggie engaged in a conversation about various animals and their feet, Breanna couldn't help but think it was a shame Adam had no intentions of becoming a father.

He showed a natural ease with Maggie, not talking down to her or at her, but rather with her. Maybe he's just on his best behavior and being kind and patient to the granddaughter of his host and hostess, she thought. That was the socially correct thing to do.

She was relieved when Savannah and Jacob Kincaid joined them at the table.

It was dusk when Breanna drove them back home. Maggie, overwhelmed by the food, fresh air and play, immediately fell asleep in the back seat.

"Thank you for letting me ride with you today," Adam said as they pulled out of the James's driveway.

"No problem," she replied.

"I noticed an old grill in the shed behind the cottage. If I get it out and clean it up, maybe you and Maggie could join me for hamburgers one evening next week."

Now was the time to draw boundaries, Breanna thought. For the time that he was renting the cottage they would share a backyard, but she had no intention of being anything more than nodding-acquaintance-type neighbors.

"Thanks, but we usually keep pretty busy between my schedule and Rachel's."

"Rachel?" In the glow of twilight his eyes appeared more silver than blue.

"Rachel is my live-in nanny," Breanna explained. "She has been my helping hand ever since I hired her two years ago."

"Must have been hard to find somebody to trust to live in your home and caretake for your child," he observed.

"Rachel was special from the first moment I met her. She came into the police department to file a complaint against an old boyfriend who was stalking her. I took the complaint and could immediately tell she was bright, good-hearted but had made the mistake of hooking up with the wrong kind of man." Breanna turned into her driveway, shut off the car engine then turned to Adam. "Having made that mistake myself, I instantly empathized with her."

"What happened with her and her boyfriend?" Adam asked.

"He caught up with her one night and beat the hell out of her, used a knife to cut up her face. He's now serving time and Rachel and I have become best of friends."

Adam reached out and placed his hand on her forearm, his gaze so intense it momentarily seemed to stop her heart. "You said you'd made the same mistake...your ex-husband...he didn't hurt you, did he?"

His hand was warm, filled with energy and far too pleasant against her cool skin. She moved and he drew back his hand as if surprised to have found himself touching her.

"You want to know if my ex-husband beat me?" she asked. "Absolutely not. He knew better than to ever lay a hand on me." She was vaguely surprised by the bitterness that rose in her voice with each word. "You asked if he ever hurt me? He promised undying love and fidelity. He played at building dreams, then he broke the promises and shattered the dreams. Did he hurt me? Unbearably…irreparably." She threw open her car door. "And now I'll just say good night." She got out of the car and slammed her door, surprised by the depth of emotions the conversation had stirred.

"Breanna," he said as he got out of the car. "I'm sorry if I upset you."

As quickly as it had swept over her, the anger died. She drew a deep, calming breath. "No, I'm sorry. I'm afraid talking about my ex puts me in a bad mood. I didn't mean to take it out on you."

She opened the back car door, unbuckled her sleeping daughter and pulled her up and into her arms, then closed the door.

"Would you like me to carry her inside for you?"

"No, thanks. I've managed on my own for the past five years. I can manage to get her inside under my own steam. Good night, Adam."

"Good night Breanna," he replied. He turned and walked across the grass toward the cottage.

It took Breanna a moment at the door as she shifted her daughter's weight from one hip to the other so she could free up a hand to dig her keys out of her purse.

Once inside she carried Maggie directly to bed. She took off the little girl's socks and shoes, then drew the sheet up around her and kissed her on the cheek.

She went back downstairs where she found a note from Rachel. The picnic with David had been a success and they had gone to the movies. She would be home later.

Breanna smiled as she read the note. She was glad things had gone well at the picnic. Rachel deserved happiness and love in her life.

She set the note aside and put a kettle of water on the stove for tea. She loved Sunday nights. Sundays and Mondays were her favorite days and nights because she was off duty. She didn't have to be back at work until Tuesday afternoon.

The phone rang and she picked it up, figuring it was probably her mother wanting to hash over the events of the day.

The recording began immediately, before Breanna even got a chance to say hello. It was the same as the night before, the woman singing ''Rock-A-Bye Baby.''

''Who is this?'' she demanded when the song had ended but the phone line remained open. ''What do you want? I really think you have the wrong number.''

''You bitch.''

The voice, gravelly deep and filled with malevolence shot a sweeping icy chill through her, but before she could make any reply, the line went dead.

The plastic of the phone felt cold in her fingers and she quickly slammed it down into the receiver, trying to shake off the chill that had taken possession of her body.

Two nights. Two phone calls. Who was making them? What did they mean? And what could they possibly have to do with her? She quickly punched *69, but got a recorded message that the number she requested was unavailable.

Like a shriek of alarm, the teakettle whistled. She jumped and stifled a scream, then quickly moved the kettle off the hot burner.

With shaking fingers, she fixed herself a cup of tea, then sat down at the kitchen table, her thoughts racing and chaotic in her mind.

A new wave of horror swept through her as she thought of her cousin Alyssa and the visions she'd seen that afternoon. Was it possible Alyssa had seen danger that concerned Breanna? Was it possible the darkness Alyssa had seen had something to do with these phone calls?

"It was a nice barbecue," Thomas James said as he helped his wife wash and dry the last of the pots and pans.

"It was, wasn't it?" Rita smiled at him, the beautiful smile that had captured his heart thirty-nine years before. That smile still had the power to make him feel like the luckiest devil on the face of the earth.

He took the last pot from her and dried it with a dish towel as she rinsed out the sink. "Bree's new neighbor seems pleasant enough," he observed.

Rita sat at the table. "Very pleasant…and very single."

"Now, honey, you know matchmaking isn't a good

idea.'' He joined her at the table. ''The kids are all grown and they have to find their own way.''

She frowned, the gesture doing nothing to diminish her beauty. ''But, Thomas, what worries me is that all of our children seem to have lost their way. Breanna clings to Maggie and to her rage over Kurt's desertion. Savannah clings to her grief as if it is her best and only friend. And Clay...he clings to his job as if it can fulfill all his needs as a man.''

He reached out and took her hand in his. ''And there's nothing we can do about it but let them find their way on their own.''

''I know.'' She sighed and squeezed his hand. He grinned and she raised a dark eyebrow. ''What are you smiling about, old man?''

''I was just thinking about what a lucky man I am. Must have been the luck of the Irish that made my car break down in front of your parents' house thirty-nine years ago.''

''And I was just a young sweet nineteen and you were such a dashing older man.''

Thomas laughed. He was eight years older than his wife. Although the eight years didn't seem so important now, he'd spent many sleepless nights at the beginning of their relationship worrying about them.

''I thought you were the most beautiful woman I'd ever seen,'' he said softly. ''And I still feel the same way.''

''Why, Mr. James, I do believe you're trying to seduce me.'' Her dark eyes gazed intently into his.

''Is it working?''

''Absolutely.'' She stood and pulled him to his feet. ''Come to bed, old man, and let this old woman show you how much you are loved.''

She might make him crazy at times with her stubbornness—she fought with him like a banshee—but he never lost sight of the fact that he was the luckiest devil on the face of the earth because Rita Birdsong loved him.

As twilight transformed into darkness, Adam remained seated on the sofa in his living room, thinking about the past day and what he'd learned about Breanna's family.

It was obvious it was a family built on the foundation of love and respect for one another. If Maggie had no other family in her life, he had a feeling the James family would be enough to make her feel secure and loved.

But she did have other family. She had Kurt's parents, who would merely add another layer of love in Maggie's life. He frowned and rubbed the center of his forehead as he thought of Breanna's reaction when the conversation had turned to her ex-husband.

What would her reaction be when he told her he was Kurt's cousin? And why did the thought of her reaction to that news bother him?

He was here at Kurt's request, to make certain Breanna and Maggie were doing okay, and they appeared to be doing just fine. All he needed to do was tell Breanna that Kurt's parents wanted a role in little Maggie's life, then leave Cherokee Corners and get back to his life in Kansas City.

With a new resolution, he turned on the lamp on the end table and picked up the phone receiver. He punched in a Kansas City number.

''Randolf residence.''

Adam recognized Miriam Walder's voice. She'd

been the housekeeper for his <u>aunt and uncle</u> for as long as he could remember.

"Miriam, it's Adam."

"Oh, Mr. Adam. It's good to hear your voice."

"It's good to hear yours, too," he replied. "Is my aunt or uncle at home?"

"Mr. <u>Edward</u> is at a meeting this evening, but Mrs. <u>Anita</u> is in the sunroom. If you'll wait just a moment, I'll take her a phone."

"Thank you, Miriam." As Adam waited, he wondered if it might not be better to give them the news that they had a grandchild when they were together. His aunt had suffered heart problems in the past and even though this news was good, it would be a shock nonetheless.

"Adam, my dear." His aunt's gentle voice filled the line. "How are you?"

"I'm fine, Aunt Anita. How are you doing?"

"All right. I'm hoping as time goes on the days and nights will get easier, that the grief will ease somewhat."

Tell her. The words boomed inside Adam's head. Tell her about Maggie. But something held him back.

"Are you having a nice getaway?" Anita asked. "You've been working so hard over the past five years Adam, and you've accomplished so much. I'm glad you decided to give yourself a little vacation. Where exactly are you?"

"I'm in a place called Cherokee Corners," he replied. "It's about one hundred fifty miles south of Tulsa."

"Whatever made you decide to go there?"

"It sounded like an interesting place, and it's rich in Native American culture."

"I never knew you were interested in that."

Adam thought of the lovely Breanna. "Neither did I. But I'm finding it more and more interesting now that I'm here."

"You'll keep in touch while you're out of town?"

"Of course. Give my love to Uncle Edward," he said. They said their goodbyes and Adam hung up.

He leaned back against the sofa and thought of his aunt. Her grief over the loss of her son was still thick…raw in her voice. But Adam realized exactly why he hadn't told her about the existence of a granddaughter.

After seeing Breanna's reaction to her experience with Kurt, he wasn't at all sure that she would allow Maggie to have anything to do with Kurt's family. The minute she mentioned Kurt, it was like a noxious poison released into her blood. It was obvious she hated him.

He had no idea what Kurt had told Breanna about his family. He knew that in the past, when it had best served his needs, Kurt had painted his parents as unloving, uncaring people. What stories had Kurt told Breanna? How black had he painted his mother and father?

Adam needed to find out what Breanna knew about his aunt and uncle. He needed to make her see that they would be a loving, caring presence in Maggie's life.

His desire to stay and get to know her a little better had nothing to do with the fact that her scent made him just a little bit dizzy, that the liquid depths of her dark eyes made him feel a little like he was drowning.

It was crazy. He had to remind himself that she was one of Kurt's women, and his job here was simply to clean up the mess Kurt had left behind…just as Adam had done so many times in the past.

His interest in Breanna had nothing to do with the fact that she was a beautiful woman, but rather with the fact that he had made a vow to a dying man.

He rubbed a hand across his lower jaw, unsurprised to feel the scrub of whisker stubble despite the fact that he'd shaved that morning. Thoughts of the day and Breanna continued to fill his head.

She'd asked him if he wanted a wife and children and he'd told her definitely not, and that was the truth. Well, a wife wouldn't be too bad…as long as she didn't want children.

Adam had seen firsthand the grief, the utter ripping and tearing children could do to their parents' hearts. He'd grown up hearing his aunt crying in the night, seeing his uncle's hollow eyes when Kurt had disappointed or hurt them yet again.

There was no way in hell Adam intended to go through that with children of his own. He'd done everything in his power to be the kind of son that would make his aunt and uncle proud, but it hadn't counted because their own son had been such a mess.

He stood, suddenly too restless to sit. If he intended to stay here a little longer and not tell Breanna exactly who he was, then he probably needed to buy some art supplies to continue the illusion of his subterfuge.

The kitchen was dark as he walked in, but light shone through the window and he knew the it was from Breanna's kitchen.

He'd noticed the night before that her kitchen window faced his with a scant eight feet or so between them. He certainly didn't want to peep, but found himself drawn to the window in spite of his good intentions.

Sure enough, her light was on, but there was no sign of her. However, what he saw outside her window fired a burst of adrenaline through him. A man stood on the top of her air-conditioning unit, framed against the house, obviously looking in.

Adam tore across his kitchen, through the living room and out his front door. He rounded the corner of the house, crashing through a bush.

The man whirled around at the noise and fell off the air conditioner. "Hey," Adam exclaimed as he raced toward him.

Adam never saw what the man used to hit him in the head. He only saw the man's arm arc out, then felt the tremendous blow that knocked him backward and to the ground.

He was vaguely aware of footsteps running away and an array of stars swimming in his head as he struggled to sit up.

"What in the hell is going on?"

The stars receded and he followed the sound of the voice to see Breanna, gun drawn and pointed at him.

"You've got to stop pointing that at me," he said, surprised that his voice seemed to be coming from some distance away. "One of these times you're going to shoot me and I'm a good guy."

The stars spun faster in his head, then blinked out and Adam knew no more.

Chapter 4

Breanna held tight to her gun and walked to where Adam lay flat on his back, his forehead bleeding profusely.

She had no idea what had happened. She'd entered her kitchen in time to see the back of a man's head at her window, then heard a commotion that had prompted her to grab her gun and check it out.

The blood on Adam's forehead didn't concern her as much as the large lump that was rising up, and the fact that he appeared to be out cold.

"Adam..." She leaned down next to him and tapped the side of his cheek. She divided her focus between him and the surrounding area.

It was obvious he hadn't done this to himself and she was aware that danger could still be anywhere, hiding in the shadows of the night.

She tapped him on the cheek again, this time a bit more forcefully. "Adam...wake up." He stirred and his eyes fluttered a couple of times, then remained open. With a groan, he sat up, his hand reaching for his head.

"We need to get you inside. Can you get up?" She wasn't about to relinquish her hold on her weapon. If he wanted some medical attention he was going to have to get up under his own steam.

"Yeah...I'm fine." He pulled himself up and to his feet, but it was obvious by his ghostly, pain-racked features that he wasn't fine. A deep moan eased from his lips.

She grabbed hold of one of his arms. "Come on, let's get you inside."

He didn't attempt to answer, but stumbled forward toward her place. The minute they entered her house, Breanna tucked her gun into her waistband, locked the front door, then led Adam into the bathroom off the foyer.

"Sit," she commanded and pointed to the stool. As he eased down, she opened the cabinet beneath the sink and pulled out a washcloth and some antiseptic cream. "What happened?" she asked as she wet the cloth.

"Somebody was looking into your kitchen window. I happened to look out my window and saw him. Ouch!" He jerked as she applied the cloth to the wound. "I ran out to see what was going on and he hit me with something."

"I think it was a broken brick. There were a couple next to the air-conditioning unit." She tried to focus on cleaning his wound and not on the fact that somebody had been looking into her house, not on the fact that Adam's body was warm and smelled so clean and male. "We should call a doctor. You were out for a minute or two. You probably have a concussion.''

"I'm fine," he replied. "I think instead of calling a doctor, you should call the cops."

"Adam, I am a cop," she replied dryly. She finished cleaning off the blood, revealing a small cut and a healthy sized goose egg. She applied some of the antiseptic cream to the wound. "I think you're going to live."

"Thanks, I was hoping that would be the prognosis." He smiled and suddenly she was aware of the small confines of the bathroom.

"Let me just get you a bandage. Head wounds are notorious for bleeding a lot." Once again she opened the cabinet under the sink and withdrew a Band-Aid. "I'm afraid cartoon characters are all I have."

He took it from her and smiled again. "I've always been fond of cartoons." He stood, still a bit unsteady on his feet.

"You put your Band-Aid on and I'll be out in the kitchen." She fled the bathroom, glad to get some distance from his overwhelming nearness. Even woozy and wounded, he was still far too attractive for her peace of mind.

And she needed to think...not about the length of Adam's dark eyelashes, not about the width of his broad chest or the evocative warmth of his skin, but why somebody would be peeking in her window.

For the first time since she'd moved into this house two years before, she walked into the kitchen and drew the curtains so they covered the window. She sat at the kitchen table and stared at the window.

Had he been there, watching her as she drank her tea? Had he peeked into other windows as well? Had he watched her as she curled up on the sofa and read or as she viewed her favorite television programs? She'd never thought of having an alarm system installed, but suddenly it didn't seem like a bad idea.

Thank goodness the bedrooms were all upstairs, making it virtually impossible for anyone to peep unless they climbed the big tree in the front yard.

Adam entered the kitchen, looking rakish with the Band-Aid across the left side of his forehead. "I feel like a pirate with a cartoon character fetish," he exclaimed as he sat at the kitchen table.

"We probably should go down to the station and make an assault report," she said.

"Is that really necessary?"

She shrugged, then asked. "Did you see what he looked like?"

"Afraid not. It was dark and I didn't have a chance to discern features or even hair color, but I can tell you he wasn't quite as tall as me…maybe five-ten or five-eleven."

Breanna jumped up and got a pad and pencil from a drawer, then returned to the table. "It's probably nothing…maybe just a teenager or a nut…but I'll just jot down a few notes. Can you tell me what kind of a build he had?"

He frowned, the frown quickly becoming a wince as one hand shot up to touch his head.

"Maybe we should do this tomorrow," she said worriedly. "You really should see a doctor."

He dropped his hand. "I'm fine. I just have one hell of a headache, but that's to be expected after being smashed in the head with a brick. Maybe some ice would help."

"Of course." She got up once again and grabbed

a dish towel from a drawer, then several ice cubes from the freezer.

She was self-consciously aware of his gaze following her movements and was grateful she hadn't yet changed into her nightshirt before the commotion had begun.

She handed him the makeshift ice pack, then again returned to the chair opposite his. He pressed the towel against his head. "You asked me about his build."

She nodded. His eyes were the purest blue she thought she'd ever seen. Like drowning pools, they seemed to beckon her closer...deeper. A flood of warmth swept through her and she stared down at her notepad, trying to remain focused on what he was saying.

"...not fat, just kind of stocky. At least, that's the impression I got before I saw stars."

"So, about five-ten or so and rather stocky." She looked at him again. "Doesn't tell us much, does it? But, as I said before, it was probably just some kid." She frowned as she thought of the phone calls she'd received. Surely the two weren't connected, or were they?

"What?" Adam leaned forward and set the ice pack on the table.

"Oh, it's nothing," she said quickly, as if by convincing him she would also convince herself.

"Breanna." He reached across the table and covered her hand with his. Pinpricks of heat sparked in her hand and shot warmth up her arm. "You have a very expressive face," he said, "and right now it's telling me that there's something else that has you worried."

It worried her that she liked the feel of his big, strong hand over hers. It bothered her that through the mere touch of his hand, she somehow felt safe... protected.

"I've gotten a couple of strange phone calls the last two nights," she said and pulled her hand from beneath his.

He leaned back, a furrow of concern creasing his forehead. "What do you mean by strange?"

She explained to him about the two calls she'd received, about the woman singing the lullaby and then earlier that night when the man had called her a bitch.

She'd thought Adam's eyes to be the clear, crisp blue of a cloudless autumn sky, but when she finished speaking his eyes were a slate blue...darker...harder.

"Have you told anyone else about the phone calls? Anyone down at the police department or any of your family?"

"No. When I got the call last night, I just assumed it was a wrong number or a silly prank." She fought against a shiver as she thought of the hatred...the utter malevolence in the man's voice as he'd said that single word.

"Can you think of anyone you might have ticked off lately?" he asked.

She smiled wryly. "Adam, I'm a cop. I tick people off on a regular basis." Her smile fell and she frowned once again. "But I can't think of anyone I've ticked off that would play a tape of a woman singing a child's lullaby, then peep into my window."

Adam stood and grabbed the makeshift ice pack that was beginning to puddle on the table. He carried it to the sink, then turned back to look at her.

"What worries me about the window peeping is

how easily the guy resorted to violence to get away. There was no warning, no hesitation when he swung that brick at my head.''

''I know,'' she said. ''That worries me, too.'' A pounding began in her head, a dull thud that threatened to intensify at any moment.

She pushed away from the table and stood. ''Adam, I'm sorry you got hurt and I really appreciate your help, but we aren't going to solve this little mystery tonight and I'm exhausted.''

Together they left the kitchen and walked out the front door and onto the porch. ''If you were a really good neighbor you'd offer to sleep with me.''

She stared at him, certain she'd misunderstood what he'd just said. ''Excuse me?''

He grinned. ''You know, so that you could wake me up every hour and look at the pupils of my eyes. Isn't that what you're supposed to do with somebody who might have a concussion? What else did you think I meant?'' His eyes held a knowing twinkle.

''I knew that's what you meant,'' she replied, wondering if her cheeks appeared as red as they felt. ''But if you're that concerned about it, I highly recommend an emergency room at one of the local hospitals.''

''I like my idea better.'' The twinkle in his eyes faded and his smile fell. ''Breanna.'' He reached out and touched her cheek with his warm fingertips. ''I'm right next door if anything happens or if you just get afraid. I can be over here in mere seconds.''

He dropped his hand, murmured a good-night, then turned and disappeared into the shadows of the night.

Breanna stepped back inside and carefully locked the front door. Gazing at her watch she realized it was after eleven.

She should go to bed. Maggie was usually an early riser and Rachel wasn't officially on duty for the next two days. Sundays, Mondays and Tuesdays were Breanna's days off, then she worked four ten-hour shifts on the other days. However, those ten-hour shifts often became twelve-or fourteen-hour shifts when she was in the middle of a case.

She climbed the stairs and checked in on Maggie before going into her own room. As she changed into her nightshirt, her four-poster bed beckoned to her, but her head was too jumbled for sleep.

Instead she shut off her bedroom light and curled up in the overstuffed chair by the window.

From this vantage point she could see part of Adam's front yard and a portion of her own. The huge oak tree that brought birdsong and the sound of scampering squirrels into her window each morning obscured the rest of the view.

She still couldn't help but believe the phone calls were some kind of crazy mistake of some kind. Why would anyone play her a tape of a woman singing a lullaby? It made absolutely no sense.

What made even less sense were the thoughts that filled her head where Adam Spencer was concerned.

Why was she wondering what it would be like to sleep with him? She knew his skin would be warm against hers, knew that his scent would surround her. By even mentioning it in jest, he'd let her know that he was attracted to her.

With a sigh of irritation she got up from the chair and stepped closer to the window. She leaned her forehead against the glass pane. What would it be like to make love to Adam?

The question came unbidden to her mind, along

with a tumble of related questions. Would he be a slow and sensual lover, relishing each touch, every caress?

Kurt had been the only lover she'd ever had, and although she'd believed herself to be deeply in love with him, she'd found their lovemaking to be vaguely unsettling...unfulfilling.

He'd always made love quickly, as if eager to get to the ultimate destination instead of enjoying the scenery along the way. She'd always been left with an emptiness inside. Would making love with Adam fill that emptiness?

She whirled away from the window and got into bed. She was thinking crazy thoughts. Anyone would think that she'd received a blow to the head that had shot all rational thought straight out her ears.

She'd only known Adam for less than two days. She knew very little about him and certainly had no idea what kind of a man he was.

Yes, you do, a small voice whispered in her head. You know he's the kind of man to put himself at risk when he suspects trouble. She reached up and rubbed her cheek in the same place he'd caressed it. You know he has a gentle touch, the voice continued.

"Shut up," she said aloud. At that moment she heard the sound of car doors shutting, then a moment later the sound of her front door opening, then closing.

Footsteps whispered against the carpeting on the stairs as Breanna reached over and turned on her bedside lamp. A second later Rachel appeared in the doorway.

"Did I wake you?" she asked. "I was trying to come in quietly."

"No, you didn't wake me." Breanna sat up and patted her bed. "Come in and tell me all about your date."

With a wide smile, Rachel flew to the bed and bounced on the mattress, looking far younger than her twenty-five years. "It was the best day and night of my life," she exclaimed.

Thoughts of Adam receded as Breanna listened to Rachel telling about her date with David. "The picnic went beautifully. We ate, then went for a walk in the park. He's so easy to talk to. We talked about anything and everything."

"I told you that you'd have a great time."

Rachel's smile was beatific. "We did. In fact, when the picnic was finished, we weren't ready to call it a day. That's when he suggested we see a movie."

"So, when are you seeing him again?"

"Next Sunday. We're going to church together, then out to dinner afterward."

"That's great," Breanna replied. "We had a bit of excitement around here tonight." She briefly told Rachel about the window peeper and Adam getting hit in the head.

"Oh, my gosh…is he all right?"

"He's fine. We iced his head and he insisted he didn't need to see a doctor. You haven't received any strange phone calls lately, have you?"

"Strange phone calls?" Rachel eyed her curiously. "What do you mean?"

"The past two nights I've gotten calls where I answer and somebody plays a tape recording of a woman singing 'Rock-A-Bye Baby.'"

Rachel gasped and one hand rose to the scar on her cheek as her eyes filled with tears of horror. "It's

Michael...it's Michael and he's calling to torment me." She burst into tears.

Breanna quickly put an arm around Rachel's shaking shoulders. "Rachel, don't cry. As far as we know Michael is still in jail. Besides, why on earth would he be playing that song to torment you?"

"Because of the baby...because of our baby." Rachel grabbed for a tissue from the box on Breanna's nightstand.

"What baby?" Breanna asked in surprise.

Rachel wiped her eyes and drew a deep breath. "When I finally got up the nerve to leave Michael, I was three months pregnant. It was the baby that gave me the strength, the courage to finally leave. I'd allowed him to be abusive to me, but I couldn't allow him to hurt our baby."

"And so you left him," Breanna said.

She nodded and dabbed at her eyes with the tissue. "Somehow he found out I was pregnant and that's when the stalking began. Three weeks later I miscarried. The doctor told me it was possibly stress related. Anyway, I told Michael there wasn't a baby, that I'd miscarried."

"But, he didn't believe you," Breanna guessed.

"He thought I'd had an abortion. That last night when he caught up with me in the grocery store parking lot, he beat me up because I'd left him, but when he cut me, he said he was doing it because I'd let a doctor cut his baby out of me." She began to cry once again.

Breanna held her close and murmured the same kind of soothing sounds she did when Maggie cried. Her heart ached with the pain of what Rachel had been through.

She let Rachel cry until her tears were finally spent, then she placed her hands firmly on Rachel's shoulders and eyed her with all the confidence she could muster.

"Okay, here's the plan. First thing in the morning I'll get on the phone and find out if Michael Rivers is still a guest of the Oklahoma Department of Corrections. If he is, we'll find out if he has access to a phone, and if he is indeed making these calls. If he is, then we'll see to it that his telephone privileges are revoked."

"And what if he's not still in jail?" Rachel asked, fear darkening her eyes.

"Then I'll find out exactly where he is and what he's up to. One thing you have to remember, Rachel. You aren't the same woman you were two years ago. You're stronger, strong enough to deal with whatever you have to."

Breanna grabbed Rachel's hand and squeezed tightly. "The next thing to remember is that you aren't alone this time. You're living with a cop and there's no way in hell I'm going to let anything happen to the best baby-sitter in the world."

A tentative laugh escaped Rachel. "Thanks, Bree."

The two women hugged, then Breanna stood and pulled Rachel to her feet. "Don't you worry about anything. We'll have some answers in the morning and will figure it all out then."

A few minutes later Breanna shut off her bedside lamp and settled into bed. Now that she knew about the baby Rachel had lost the phone calls made more sense. They were sick…and wicked, but they made sense.

It had to be Michael. He was about five foot ten

and although he'd been on the thin side when he'd been convicted, Breanna knew the starchy prison food could quickly transform a thin man into a stocky one.

He'd been sentenced to three to five years and that had been almost two years ago. With good time served he could conceivably be out now.

It was a proven fact that he had a penchant for violence. He wouldn't have thought twice about hitting Adam over the head to save his own skin.

If he was out then he was probably on parole and hunting down Rachel, peeping in windows, would get that parole revoked in a second.

It has to be Michael, she thought. That was the only thing that made sense. If it wasn't Michael and the phone calls weren't meant for Rachel, but rather for herself, then it didn't make sense. And things that didn't make sense worried Breanna. They worried her a lot.

Chapter 5

"Tell the truth, Adam. You like taking care of my women after I dump them because it allows you to get close to women who otherwise would never give you the time of day. Face it, you're boring and you'll always be second choice when I'm around."

Adam bolted upright in bed, his heart thudding rapidly. The image of Kurt faded as sleep fell away. Sunshine streamed into the small bedroom, letting Adam know he'd slept later than usual.

He raised a hand to his forehead, pleased to discover the goose egg from the night before had diminished to a small lump.

As he got out of bed, he thought about the dream he'd had just before awakening. It wasn't so much a dream as it was a memory…a painful memory of the fight he and Kurt had had the last time they'd seen each other before Kurt's accident.

Adam had been giving Kurt hell for his treatment

of his latest girlfriend, a young woman named <u>Renata</u>. Kurt had gone out with her three times, finally managing to sweet talk her into his bed. He hadn't called or spoken to her after his night of pleasure.

Renata had called Adam, distraught. She'd begged him to talk to Kurt, to see what she'd done wrong, how she could fix it. It was obvious her heart was broken, and Adam had confronted Kurt and an argument had ensued.

A few minutes later, Adam stood beneath a hot shower spray and resolutely shoved thoughts of Kurt away.

Instead, thoughts of Breanna blossomed in his head. He'd actually attempted flirting with her the night before with his little comment about her sleeping with him. He had no idea what had possessed him. He had no intention of forming any kind of permanent relationship in his life.

He shut off the shower and dried off. There was no denying the fact that he was intensely drawn to Breanna on a physical level. Her scent enticed him, the feel of her skin intoxicated him and the thought of tasting her lips electrified him.

However, to follow through on his physical attraction to her, knowing he would be offering her only a few nights of pleasure and nothing more, made him no better than Kurt.

Physical attraction aside, he was concerned about Breanna. The incident last night with the peeper had been bad enough, but coupled with the odd phone calls she'd received, he couldn't help but be concerned.

He pulled on a pair of jean shorts and a polo shirt, then went into the kitchen to make some coffee. He was surprised to see it was after nine. He'd definitely slept in.

He poured himself a cup of the fresh-brewed coffee and carried it through the tiny living room and out the front door.

It felt odd not to be heading for his office, where phones rang, faxes transmitted and businesses depended on his firm to keep their books straight.

He couldn't remember the last time he'd sat and enjoyed a cup of coffee with the pleasures of a spring morning surrounding him. Most mornings he was up and at the office by six or six-thirty.

The sounds of an awakened neighborhood filled the air. A dog barked cheerfully in the distance as a bird sang a melodic tune overhead.

Adam's place in Kansas City was an apartment at the top of a high-rise building. He never heard neighborhood noises and now found himself enjoying the novelty of utter relaxation.

A slam of a door sounded from Breanna's place and he looked over to see Maggie exiting, her arms laden with a variety of items. She deposited her load in the shade of the big oak tree, then went back into the house only to return a moment later with another armful of things.

Adam sipped his coffee and watched curiously as she made three more trips in and out. By the time she was finished it appeared she'd brought every toy she owned from her room to the front yard.

She spread a sheet on the ground and began to organize the items on the sheet. As she worked, he could hear her singing. Although he couldn't quite make out the song, he found the sound of her sweet, childish voice infinitely charming.

He finished his coffee and set the cup on the porch. At that moment she saw him. "Hi, Adam." She waved at him with a bright, friendly smile. "Come on over."

Why not, he thought. He got up and ambled over to her. "I'm playing house," she said. "Wanna play?"

He was going to decline, but a wistfulness in her eyes called to him. "All right," he agreed. "What do you want me to do?"

"First you have to say hi to Mr. Bear." She gestured to the big brown stuffed bear that sat in a doll's high chair.

"How do you do, Mr. Bear?" Adam shook one furry paw. "It's nice to make your acquaintance."

"He says it's nice to make your 'quaintance, too. This is my table," she said and pointed to an overturned cardboard box. "Would you like to have a cup of coffee?"

"That sounds nice." He sat cross-legged on the sheet at the end of the box.

Maggie dug into a little pink duffel bag and withdrew a plastic cup and saucer. "Be careful," she said as she placed them before him. "It's very hot."

"Thank you." Adam pretended to sip from the cup. "You make great coffee."

Maggie's little smile faded as she gazed at him. "You have a boo-boo on your forehead. Does it hurt?"

"Only a little," he replied.

To his surprise she walked up to him, placed a tiny hand on each of his cheeks and soundly kissed his boo-boo. "There," she said with obvious satisfaction.

"Kisses are like magical Band-Aids. They take the hurt away."

As she stepped away from him, Adam's heart expanded in a way it never had before. Oh, Kurt, he thought. You have no idea what you missed in not knowing this sweet little girl.

"Do you like ice cream?" Maggie asked as she set a cup and saucer in front of Mr. Bear.

"Sure. It's one of my most favorite things to eat."

"Alyssa has an ice-cream parlor in her bed-and-breakfast. She has chocolate marshmallow ice cream."

"I like strawberry," Adam replied.

"She has that, too." Maggie grabbed a cup and saucer for herself and sat at the opposite end of the box from Adam. "My friends, their daddies take them for ice cream sometimes." She sighed heavily. "But I don't have a daddy to take *me* for ice cream."

"Maybe I could take you for ice cream some time." The words left his mouth before he'd thought them through. What was he doing? The last thing he wanted was to become personally involved in Maggie's life. The last thing he wanted was to have any sort of emotional investment where she was concerned.

Her gray eyes sparkled brightly and she clapped her hands together. "For real? Do you promise?"

How could Adam deny her? "Sure, I promise."

"That would make me happy."

At that moment Adam saw Breanna seated on the front porch. He wondered how much of the exchange between him and Maggie she'd heard. "I think I'll go say hi to your mommy now," he said.

"Okay."

Adam pulled himself up and ambled to the porch, unable to help but notice how lovely Breanna looked in a colorful sundress that emphasized her bronze skin tones and dark eyes.

"Good morning," he said.

"I see you survived the night," she said and motioned to the wicker chair next to where she sat. Her eyes were dark, fathomless and Adam wished he knew what thoughts were flittering through her mind.

"Yeah, I survived."

"You realize you just made a fatal mistake."

He eyed her curiously. "What are you talking about?"

"You actually sat down and drank a cup of pretend coffee with Maggie. Now she'll expect you to play every time she sees you outside."

"I suppose there are worse mistakes I could make," he replied.

"You realize she won't forget that you mentioned taking her for ice cream. Kids have amazing memories and Maggie can be as tenacious as a pit bull."

"I made a promise...and I don't break my promises."

"How refreshing, a man who doesn't break promises," she said dryly. But, before he could reply, she continued. "Actually, I was going to go over to your place to talk to you this morning. I think maybe we've solved the mystery of the phone calls and the peeper."

"Really?" He listened with interest as she told him about Michael Rivers and Rachel and their suspicions that it was him who had been making the calls and spying on Rachel. "What have you found out about him?'' he asked when she was finished explaining things.

She frowned. ''He's out of jail. He got out a month ago. Apparently he moved to Sycamore Ridge, a little town just north of here.'' She gestured to the cordless phone on the chair next to her. ''I'm waiting to hear from his parole officer to find out exactly where he is and what he's doing.''

''Then what?''

''Then I go have a little talk with him. If he did these things, then he'll be back in jail so fast his head will spin.'' Her jaw was set with fierce determination.

''You won't go talk to him alone, right? You have a partner or somebody who goes with you on things like this?''

Logically, he knew she was a cop, trained to encounter dangerous criminals and situations, but the thought of her confronting the man who'd hit him in the head with a brick, caused a stir of anxiety to fill him.

''I have a wonderful partner named Abe Solomon. He's a great guy and I trust him with my life.'' Her affection for her partner was evident in her voice.

Adam was surprised to feel a flicker of an alien emotion wing through him…an emotion that felt remarkably like jealousy. ''So, you and your partner…you're tight?''

She nodded. ''You have to be tight with your partner when you're a cop. It's kind of like a marriage…without the heartache and without the sex.'' Her cheeks pinkened slightly.

''You've been partners with this Abe for a long time?''

''For almost five years. He's planning on retiring

in the next year or so and I hate to even think about it. It will be like losing my favorite uncle.''

A wave of relief rushed through him. A favorite uncle...retirement...Abe Solomon was obviously considerably older than Breanna and definitely not a love interest.

What do you care, he mentally chided himself. She isn't a love interest of yours, either. She had been one of Kurt's women and that was the end of the story.

"I'd better get back," he said and stood, suddenly needing to be away from her.

"How's the painting? Have you started anything yet?''

He stared at her blankly for a moment, then remembered. "Oh...the painting...no, I haven't started on anything. I'm waiting for inspiration to hit." He stepped off the porch. "You'll let me know what you find out about this Michael Rivers guy?"

"Sure," she agreed. She stood and he couldn't help but notice how the dress clung to her curves.

"I'll see you later." He turned to escape, but nearly ran into Maggie, who looked up at him with a sweet smile.

"How about we go get some ice cream tonight?" she asked.

He wanted to say no. He felt off balance, torn between his attraction to Breanna and the knowledge that he didn't want to be attracted to her. But Maggie's eyes held the eagerness of anticipation and no matter what his personal baggage, he couldn't disappoint her.

He looked questioningly at Breanna, who frowned thoughtfully. "Of course, when I told Maggie I'd take her for ice cream, I intended you to go along as well," he said.

"I wouldn't allow it any other way," she replied.

"Mommy, you can't say no," Maggie exclaimed as if horrified by the very thought. "We'll have ice cream and it will be such fun!"

Breanna gazed at her daughter and in her eyes Adam saw the enormous love of mother for child. She looked from Maggie to Adam and he had the feeling that she felt just like he did…somehow reluctant to go and yet equally reluctant to disappoint Maggie.

"I suppose we could go for ice cream after dinner tonight," she finally said.

"Yea!" Maggie jumped up and down and clapped her hands together.

"Shall we make it about six or so?" he asked.

"That would be fine."

"I'll see you then." It's just ice cream, he told himself as he walked back to his house. It wasn't like he'd invited Breanna for a date or anything like that. This was about buying ice cream for Maggie.

As he picked up his cup and went back into the cottage, he wondered why it somehow seemed so much more complicated than just an ice-cream cone.

It was ridiculous. Breanna stood before the mirror in her bedroom and looked at her reflection. This was the third outfit she'd pulled on just to go get ice cream.

First the shorts had been too short, then the blouse had been all wrong. Now she wondered why she was spending so much time worrying about what she had on. She finally settled on a salmon-colored "skort" and matching sleeveless blouse. Brown sandals adorned her feet and although she had put on a little mascara, she refused to put on lipstick. That would make it too much like a date.

Checking her watch, she realized it was almost six. She left her bedroom. "Maggie, it's almost time to go." She found her daughter sitting on the foot of her bed putting on her shoes.

"This is going to be fun, isn't it, Mommy?" Maggie's eyes shone brightly. "It's gonna be just like having a daddy."

Breanna's heart constricted. More and more frequently Maggie mentioned the lack of a father in her life and Breanna ached with the void her daughter felt, a void she didn't have the power to fill.

"Maggie, you know Adam is just a neighbor, not your daddy," Breanna replied.

"I know. But I can pretend…just to myself."

"But no amount of pretending is going to make him your daddy."

"Mommy, I know that," Maggie replied with a touch of impatience. She got her last shoe on and stood. "I just sometimes wish I had a daddy."

As they walked down the stairs, Breanna thought about Kurt and her heart grew hard and cold. How could a man so easily walk away from parenthood?

He'd left her when she was seven months pregnant, confessing that he'd jumped into the marriage and wasn't ready to be a husband or a father. She tried never to think about the other hurtful things he'd said when he'd walked away.

He'd left her a post office box number in Platte City, Missouri, and told her to send him the divorce papers there.

She'd sent him the divorce papers and every year

at Christmastime she'd sent him a picture of the little girl he'd sired. She'd never heard a word from him and she hated him for not being man enough to be a father, and hated herself for choosing so badly when it came to a husband and father for her baby.

As she and Maggie left the house, she shoved away thoughts of Kurt, knowing that thinking about him always put her in a foul mood.

She and Maggie sat in the wicker chairs on the porch, waiting for six o'clock and Adam to appear. Maggie's face held the sweetness of childish anticipation as she wiggled in the chair.

Breanna leaned back and thought about that morning. As she'd sat here and watched Adam with Maggie, a bittersweet pang had exploded in her heart. As he'd pretended to drink Maggie's coffee she'd seen what life might have been like for her daughter if Maggie had had a daddy.

If Maggie had a daddy, there would be father-daughter moments that Breanna couldn't provide for her child. But Adam Spencer couldn't provide those moments, either.

He'd made it clear he wanted no children and he was only in town on a temporary basis. Besides, she wasn't in the market for a husband. She'd never again trust her own judgment where a man was concerned and refused to go through the process of finding not only a good man for herself, but a good stepfather for Maggie as well.

Speaking of men... Adam's door opened and he stepped outside, looking far too handsome in a pair of worn jeans and a short-sleeved blue pullover shirt.

"Adam!" Maggie cried as she jumped down from the chair. "We're ready for ice cream!"

"Good, so am I," he replied with a warm smile that made sunbursts of smile lines radiate from the outside corners of his eyes. His smile remained as he gazed at Breanna. "You want me to drive or can we walk?"

"Walk!" Maggie exclaimed.

Breanna stood and shrugged. "It's about ten blocks to the square, but it's a nice evening for a walk."

"Then walk it is," he replied.

Breanna and Adam fell into step side by side on the sidewalk as Maggie danced just ahead of them. The approach of evening brought a slight breeze that was pleasant and filled with the scent of spring flowers.

"Beautiful evening," he observed, as if reading her mind.

"We'd better enjoy them. Summer gets hot in Cherokee Corners. But, of course, you probably won't be here to suffer the heat of the late summer months."

"That's true. By July I'll probably be cooped up in my office in Kansas City, all dreams of being an artist dashed by a lack of any real talent."

She cast him a sideways glance, noting how his blue shirt brought out the clear blue of his eyes. "You don't sound too upset about the prospect."

"What? Of being back in my office? To tell you the truth, I like my work as the owner of an accounting firm. I know most people think account work is boring, but I like not having surprises when it comes to my livelihood." He smiled again. "I'm sure your work in law enforcement is much more exciting."

"You'd be surprised at how much drudge work there is." She felt herself relaxing with each step they took and the easiness of the conversation flowing between them. "Much of my time is spent writing reports and reading files."

"But you work a prostitution detail. Doesn't that get a little dicey?"

"It hasn't yet," she replied. "Maggie, wait for us before crossing the street," she instructed, then looked back at him. "I've never had any problems working undercover prostitution. Sure, some of the men we arrest get really angry, but I've always got plenty of backup and I don't do any of the real arresting on those nights."

They caught up with Maggie, who was waiting for them at the corner. "Hold my hand," Breanna said and held out her hand to her daughter.

"I want to hold Adam's hand," Maggie replied and smiled up at Adam.

Adam looked surprised, but took Maggie's hand in his and the three of them crossed the street. "When you were little, did your mommy make you hold her hand when you crossed a street?" Maggie asked.

"Always," Adam replied.

"And did your daddy take you for ice cream?"

"Not that I remember. My daddy died when I was eleven years old," Adam said.

"That's sad," Maggie replied. "We don't know where my daddy is. He went away before I was borned and we haven't seen him since."

"So what kind of ice cream is everyone going to get?" Breanna asked, uncomfortable with the conversation's direction and attempting to change the subject.

"Strawberry," Adam replied, the expression on his face letting her know he knew what she was doing.

"Chocolate marshmallow with some sprinkles on

top,'' Maggie exclaimed. ''What about you, Mommy? What kind are you going to get?''

Breanna pretended to frown thoughtfully. ''I don't know…maybe some artichoke ice cream.''

Maggie's giggles rode the breeze. ''That's silly, Mommy.''

''Nobody eats artichoke ice cream,'' Adam added.

Breanna laughed. ''Then maybe I'll just get vanilla.''

As Maggie ran ahead, Breanna felt Adam's gaze lingering on her. ''What?'' she asked.

''Vanilla ice cream? That surprises me. I'd have figured you for something more exotic, more adventurous.''

She laughed again. ''Then you definitely have the wrong impression about me. I'm neither exotic nor adventurous. I'm just a vanilla ice cream kind of woman.''

She fought a sudden edge of bitterness as she remembered that had been the problem with her marriage. Kurt had been disappointed to discover she was a vanilla ice cream kind of woman.

They entered the city square and the red-and-pink awning of the ice-cream parlor came into view. The ice-cream parlor comprised the bottom floor of the three-story building. The upper two floors were The Redbud Bed and Breakfast, so named after the state tree.

Tall, round glass-topped tables dotted the interior, but Maggie clambered up on a stool at the counter, behind which Alyssa stood dipping up ice cream and old-fashioned charm in equal doses. Breanna slid onto the stool next to Maggie and Adam took the one next to Breanna.

"Hey, what have we here?" Alyssa leaned across the counter and tapped Maggie on the nose. "I'll bet somebody is ready for a two-story chocolate marshmallow cone."

Maggie giggled. "Yup," she exclaimed. "And Mommy wants vanilla and Adam wants strawberry."

Alyssa smiled at Breanna, then at Adam. "How are you two doing?"

They small-talked for a few minutes, then Alyssa served them their cones. Maggie got hers first, then Breanna and finally Adam. As Alyssa handed Adam his, her smile wavered slightly and Breanna thought she saw a whisper of worry darken her cousin's eyes. It was there only a moment, then gone.

As they ate their ice cream, they visited both with Alyssa and with the people who came into the shop. But Breanna couldn't stop thinking about that look she'd seen in Alyssa's eyes.

"Would you mind watching Maggie," Breanna asked Adam when they'd finished their cones. "I'd like to talk to Alyssa alone for just a minute."

"Sure," he agreed. "Come on, Maggie, let's go outside and you can tell me what kind of stores there are around here."

When they were gone, Breanna leaned over the counter and eyed her cousin intently. "You felt something when you handed Adam his cone," she said. "And don't try to deny it. I saw it in your eyes."

"It was nothing really," Alyssa protested. "Just confusion...I felt confusion. Honestly, Bree, I don't think it's anything to worry about...at least where Adam is concerned." She frowned.

"But...?" Breanna pressed.

Alyssa's brown eyes seemed to grow darker. "I

still have a feeling of something bad happening...something horrid." She forced a laugh and waved her hand as if to dismiss the entire topic. "I've been feeling off-kilter for days now. I can't figure it out."

"Is there anything I can do to help?" Breanna asked.

Alyssa smiled and shook her head. "Unfortunately, no." She grabbed a sponge and wiped down the counter. "I keep thinking maybe the moon is in a weird phase or my hormones are out of whack."

"You aren't pregnant, are you?"

Alyssa laughed. "That would be a little difficult since I'm not even dating anyone right now." She reached across the counter and touched Breanna's hand. "Just be careful, Bree. I've got a bad feeling and I don't know what it's about or who it concerns."

"I've got to go," Breanna said, worried by Alyssa's warning and realizing her daughter was outside with a man she knew little about, even though she could see them from where she stood.

"Call me," Alyssa said as Breanna ran out the door.

She approached where Adam and Maggie were seated on a bench. Maggie was pointing to various shops and chatting like a magpie and Adam had a bemused smile on his face.

He stood as she approached. "I now know which store sells the best toys, who has the cutest clothes and what clerks are cranky."

"I told him about Mrs. Clairborn," Maggie explained. "I told him she was a witch!"

"That's not nice to say," Breanna replied, although

secretly she agreed with her daughter. Katherine Clairborn was a mean-spirited witch.

But her head was still filled with Alyssa's warning. Be careful. Be careful of what? Of Adam? Now that she thought about it, she'd received the first strange phone call the night he'd moved in next door. Coincidence? Or something more sinister?

"Breanna?"

She flushed, realizing she'd been staring at him. "We'd better start back home. It's getting dark."

"Are you okay?" he asked softly as they headed for home.

"Fine," she replied in distraction. It made no sense for Adam to have made those calls to her, and he certainly hadn't hit himself over the head with the brick the night before. It was all so confusing.

"I'm worried about Alyssa," she finally said, watching as Maggie hopscotched ahead of them.

"What about her?" he asked.

She frowned, wondering how much to say, how foolish it might be to trust him given Alyssa's words of caution. But, no matter what her head said, her heart told her he was a man who could be trusted.

"Alyssa is special…or cursed, depending on what school of thought you come from."

"I don't understand. What do you mean?"

They walked slowly as night fell, casting shadows outside of the pools of light created by the streetlamps they passed.

"Alyssa has suffered visions since she was a small child."

"You mean like psychic stuff?" Even in the darkening of night she could see his eyes holding a hint of incredulity.

"You can believe it or not, but I can tell you that it's very real," she said defensively.

"I have an open mind when it comes to the possibility of such things," he replied. "Is that what happened at the barbecue the day I met her?"

"Yes. Usually immediately after having a vision she falls unconscious for several minutes." They turned onto the street where their houses were mid-block.

"Did she have some sort of vision about me?" he asked.

She shot him a quick sideways look. He almost sounded guilty. "Why do you ask? Do you have something to hide?"

He laughed, but she thought it sounded rather forced. "Only the usual human weaknesses. I just figured if Alyssa had a vision of my unexpected demise, then I should know so I can get my things in order."

Maybe I'm reading too much into Alyssa's warning and seeing boogeymen where there are none, Breanna thought to herself. "Actually, Alyssa did warn me to be careful. She isn't getting any specific visions, but she has some bad feelings."

"About you and Maggie?" All laughter was gone from his voice.

"She isn't sure who or what it's about. Maggie...slow down," she exclaimed.

"Does she get these bad feelings often?"

Breanna sighed and fought against a wave of anxiety that suddenly threatened to overwhelm her. "The last time she had these kinds of bad feelings, my brother-in-law crashed his car through the guard rail of the Sequoya Bridge. He drowned in the Cherokee River."

"You don't think her bad feelings now have anything to do with the phone calls you've been receiving, do you?" He placed a hand on her arm and they stopped in place. His eyes held her gaze intently. "What did you find out about Michael Rivers?"

A blood-curdling scream rent the air.

"Maggie!" The scream ripped through Breanna's heart as she ran toward the house.

Maggie stood on the sidewalk and pointed to the big oak tree, her eyes huge and her lower lip trembling. "Look, Mommy."

Hanging from the branches was a pink plastic cradle. On the branch just beneath it, strung by a noose around his neck, hung Mr. Bear.

Chapter 6

Instinctively Adam scooped Maggie up into his arms and pressed her head against his neck in an attempt to shield her from the sight of her beloved stuffed bear.

''Rachel,'' Breanna whispered softly and ran to the front door. Adam watched as she fumbled in her purse for her keys and her gun.

A wave of helpless frustration raked through him as he fought his desire to grab the gun from Breanna and go inside. He wanted to protect her from whatever horror or danger that might be in the house.

Maggie wept against his neck. He patted her back, his gaze intent on the front door as he willed Breanna to reappear unharmed.

When the bough breaks, the cradle will fall, and down will come baby, cradle and all. The words from the old standard lullaby played and replayed through his head.

He glanced back at the tree with its gruesome ornamentation. It took a sick mind to do something like that...a twisted, sick mind.

Relief flooded through him as Breanna stepped out onto the porch. "She's not here and it doesn't look like anything has been disturbed inside."

"Mommy, can we get Mr. Bear down?" Maggie asked as she raised her tear-streaked face. "He doesn't like it up there."

"We can't take him down right now, honey. We're going to let Uncle Clay look at him first," Breanna said. Adam noticed she'd brought a cordless phone with her out of the house.

"Besides," Adam said, "maybe Mr. Bear was up in that tree looking for a bee's nest filled with honey."

"Bears like honey," Maggie said softly. Her lower lip trembled ominously. "But, Mr. Bear is so scared."

Adam sat down on the porch and cuddled her on his lap as Breanna sat next to him and began to make phone calls.

She called Rachel's cell phone first and reassured herself that Rachel was really okay. Apparently the young woman had left the house with friends soon after the three of them had left.

Breanna then called her brother, Clay, and her sister, Savannah. By the time she'd finished making her calls, Maggie had fallen asleep in Adam's arms.

"Want me to take her?" Breanna asked.

"No, she's fine," he replied. He'd never held a sleeping child in his arms before and the utter trust that Maggie had displayed in him by allowing herself to fall asleep touched him. Besides, he enjoyed the sweet smell of her, the snuggly warmth of her little body against his.

"I don't want to take her up to her room until Clay has a chance to look things over. When we left here to get ice cream, Mr. Bear was on Maggie's bed."

"So somebody got into your house." A rush of anger filled Adam.

"The back door lock is broken," she replied.

"Why don't you have an alarm system?" Adam asked. "I would think as a cop you'd have one."

She sighed. "This is a small town, Adam. I only know a handful of people who have alarm systems. I've never had a problem, never felt afraid..." Her voice trailed off.

He wondered if she'd been able to say "until now."

For a few moments they sat silent, the surrounding night silent as well, as if holding its breath in anticipation of what might come next.

"What did you find out about Michael Rivers?" he asked.

"I spoke to his parole officer and got his address. The parole officer said he's doing quite well, has a full-time job and is keeping his appointments. He's even gone through an anger management program."

"But that doesn't mean he isn't trying to terrify Rachel," Adam said.

"No, it doesn't. I had planned on getting my partner to drive to Sycamore Ridge with me tomorrow to meet with the parole officer and talk to Michael, but apparently Abe is out of town."

Before Adam could reply, a car roared down the street and into Breanna's driveway. Rita was out the passenger door and on the porch before Thomas had shut off the engine.

"Savannah called and explained everything," she said as Adam and Breanna stood. "We thought we'd come and take Maggie home with us." Rita looked at the tree, then turned back to them, her dark eyes glittering in the silvery moonlight. "Perhaps it is Raven Mocker come to take a life."

"Don't start with Indian ghost stories," Thomas said to his wife as he held out his arms to take the sleeping Maggie from Adam. He looked at Breanna. "We'll keep her with us for a couple of days. I put in a call to Glen and told him to get the guys on the force on this."

"Dad, you didn't need to call the chief," Breanna protested. At that moment another car and a van sped down the street toward them.

"We'll get this little one out of here," Thomas said. "Call us in the morning." He and Rita went back to their car as Savannah and Clay arrived on the scene.

Clay said nothing, but immediately pulled out a pad and a pen and gazed up at the tree. Savannah walked over to where Adam and Breanna stood. She gave her sister a kiss on the cheek, then offered a small smile to Adam. "Nothing like a little excitement to top off an evening, right?"

"I could live with a little less excitement," Adam replied.

They all turned as a patrol car pulled up against the curb. A big, burly man stepped out of the driver door and a second officer got out of the passenger side. Adam instantly felt Breanna's tension level rise.

"That's Chief Glen Cleberg," she said softly as she left the porch to greet her boss.

"What have we got here?" Cleberg's voice was like a boom of thunder in the otherwise silent night. He placed his meaty hands on his hips and stared up at the tree, then eyed Breanna with dark, beady eyes. "Looks like you've managed to stir up somebody."

In that single instant, Adam decided he didn't much like the chief of police. He joined Breanna, fighting a sudden impulse to throw his arm around her shoulder in a show of solidarity.

"I can't imagine what I would have done to instigate this," Breanna replied. Cleberg grunted.

Adam decided to step into the conversation. "Adam Spencer," he said and held out his hand to the chief. "I'm staying in the cottage next door."

"Haven't seen you around town," Cleberg said as he gave Adam's hand a firm shake.

"I've only been here a couple of days," Adam replied.

"Adam's an artist. He's staying here for a while to soak up some of the Native American culture," Breanna explained.

Glen frowned, the gesture creating a deep furrow in his broad brow. "Hope you don't think this kind of nonsense is normal in our town."

"Not at all. From what I've seen, Cherokee Corners is a charming place."

Glen grunted again, this time a grunt that implied satisfaction. He looked at Breanna once more. "You want to tell me about this?"

Adam remained silent as Breanna explained about the phone calls, the incident with the peeper and her suspicions that it might be Michael Rivers trying to terrorize Rachel.

"I thought he was in prison," Glen said.

"He's been out for a month. He's living in Sycamore Ridge," Breanna replied.

"That little punk better not be coming into my town and pulling any stunts." Glen drew a deep breath and looked back at the tree, where Clay had finished taking pictures and was in the process of climbing up to remove the items from the branches.

He looked back at Breanna. "You know there's not a lot we can do about a couple of phone calls and a Peeping Tom that nobody got a good look at."

"What about this?" Adam gestured to the tree.

Glen shrugged. "I suppose we could arrest whoever did it on a trespass charge, maybe stretch it to vandalism, but I got to tell you, we don't really have the manpower to follow up on this." He raked a big hand through his salt-and-pepper hair. "The town has grown faster than our police department, and unfortunately more people means more crime."

"I know how understaffed we are," Breanna said. "I hadn't intended to bother you with this. Dad shouldn't have called you."

"He was right to call me. I need to know what's going on with my officers."

"Whoever did this got into Breanna's house," Adam told the chief. "She said the back door lock has been broken."

"Why in the hell didn't you tell me that to begin with," he replied with more than a touch of irritation. "Savannah…Joseph, get inside and clear the house. The perp was inside at some point."

"I already checked the house," Breanna said.

Cleberg frowned. "Maybe you missed him. Maybe we'll get lucky and he's still in there. I'm in the mood for an arrest tonight."

Breanna's sister and the officer who had arrived with Chief Cleberg drew their weapons and entered the front door. By this time Clay had retrieved the items from the tree and had placed them in paper bags. He drew off his gloves and joined them.

"I might be able to pull off some fingerprints on the plastic of the cradle and if I'm lucky maybe some fiber evidence or something off Mr. Bear," he said.

Breanna frowned. "Be careful with Mr. Bear. Maggie will be devastated to learn that he's not here."

Clay nodded. "There doesn't seem to be any footprint impressions around the base of the tree. The ground is too dry and the grass too thick." He held up the two paper bags. "I'm going to put these in my van, then try to lift some prints around the back door lock."

"Looks like you Jameses have this scene under control. When Joseph finishes up, we'll be on our way. Make sure you write up a report on this," Cleberg said to Breanna.

A few minutes later as Joseph and the chief were leaving, Rachel arrived home. Adam watched as Breanna hugged her.

"Go pack a bag," Breanna instructed her. "I don't want you staying here for the next couple of days until we can sort this all out."

Savannah walked up and grabbed Rachel by the arm. "You can stay with me, Rachel. I've got plenty of room and would enjoy your company."

Rachel looked shell-shocked as Savannah led her

into the house to pack her things. It didn't take them long, then together they left.

Adam and Breanna went into the house where Clay was just finishing up dusting the back door. "A lot of smudges," he said, "and not a single clear print or partial. I'm ready to take a look at Maggie's room."

Adam followed brother and sister through the living room and up the stairs to Maggie's room. Adam glanced across the hall and into the room he suspected was Breanna's.

Decorated in earth tones with splashes of sky blue accents, the room emanated peace and serenity. The bed was rumpled and unmade and a vision flashed in Adam's mind…a vision of a doe-eyed Breanna, her body warm and supple with slumber.

He yanked his gaze away from the room, afraid his visions would careen out of control. Instead he turned and watched as Clay examined the room with the eyes of an expert crime scene investigator.

Adam found himself entranced by the childhood magic that surrounded him. This was a place of innocence, of sweet dreams and fairy tales. It smelled of Maggie, that curious blend of peaches and sunshine.

But Adam knew better than to be fooled by the aura of innocence. Children were like ticking time bombs, just waiting for the trigger that would detonate a heartful of sorrow for their parents.

He'd just about decided while they were having ice cream to tell Breanna who he was and why he was here. He'd also made the decision to call his aunt and uncle and tell them about Maggie. But this changed everything. He wasn't going to do anything until they got to the bottom of who was tormenting Breanna. Until this mess was cleared up, he intended to go nowhere and tell nobody anything.

Clay spent several moments just looking around the room, then turned to Breanna. "Are you certain Mr. Bear was in here before you left the house?"

Breanna frowned and raked a hand through her long, shiny hair. "I thought so…but now I'm not so sure."

"Is it possible she left him outside after she played house earlier?" Adam asked.

"I don't know…I guess it's possible," she admitted hesitantly.

"Bree, I don't want to tear up this room looking for evidence of an intruder, given the fact that nobody has been hurt and you believe this all has to do with Rachel," Clay said.

"I don't want you to tear up the room," she replied. "It would upset Maggie, but it would definitely upset the chief if you use the lab for something like this."

"I'll dust the cradle for fingerprints and let you know what I find. There isn't much else I can do here."

The three of them left the bedroom and went back downstairs to the front door. Clay leaned over and kissed his sister on her forehead, nodded to Adam, then left.

"A man of few words," Adam observed.

She nodded. "Clay has always been the silent type. Mom worries about him because he has no life outside of his work."

"It must be fascinating work."

"He keeps busy. He's only one of three crime scene investigators." She looked around in distraction.

Adam wasn't sure whether she expected him to leave, or wanted him to stay. He hated to leave her alone, knew that despite her calm facade the sight of Mr. Bear and the cradle had shaken her up badly.

"We need to see about bracing up that back door until you can get the lock fixed," he said.

"You're right." She frowned, suddenly looking vulnerable and exhausted. She sat in one of the chairs at the table.

"Why don't you put on some coffee and I'll go check in the shed. I think there are some boards in there we can use," he suggested.

"You don't mind? I mean, you don't mind staying for a little while?" she asked.

Mind? If he could, he'd stay the night, hold her in his arms and keep her safe. If he could, he'd kiss away the worry on her brow, stroke the tension from her cheek. He'd make love to her so sweetly, so gently, she'd forget about everything but being in his arms.

Stupid thoughts, he scoffed inwardly. "Not at all," he replied. "I'll just go get that lumber."

He went through the broken back door and with the aid of the back porch light, entered the small shed. What was he thinking of? Why would a woman who had married a man like Kurt ever want anything remotely romantic from a man like him?

"You've always wanted to be me." Kurt's voice filled his head. "You've always wished you were my parents' son, you've always wished you had my life and you've always wanted my women."

Adam frowned with irritation and pulled out a

board that could be used to brace the back door.
"Shut up," he muttered to the ghost in his head.

He wanted to dismiss the words that Kurt had once
said to him, but somehow, in a deep, dark place in
his heart, he was desperately afraid that they were
true.

Breanna was grateful for Adam's presence as she
made a pot of coffee. She had never spent a night
alone in the house. She'd always had the company of
her daughter and now the silence pressed in on
her...the empty silence devoid of Maggie's very
breath.

She'd seen a lot of terrible things in her short career
as a vice cop, but nothing had prepared her for the
sight of Mr. Bear hanging from the tree. She was both
angry and more than a little bit afraid. What did it all
mean? Why would somebody do something like that?

"I think I found the perfect board," Adam said as
he came through the back door. "I can brace it against
the cabinet, then just hammer in a couple of nails into
the wall. After you get the lock fixed, I can patch the
nail holes for you."

"A jack-of-all-trades," she said.

He grinned. "And master of none."

As he got to work on the back door, she poured
them each a cup of coffee, then sat down at the table
and watched him work.

She could smell him, that male scent that she
found so attractive. It was funny, although she didn't
miss Kurt, there were little, silly things she missed
about having a male in the house...like the fragrance
of minty shaving cream lingering in her bathroom,

or a sleepy early-morning cuddle against a warm, strong body.

She missed pouring two cups of coffee instead of one in the mornings, missed the small talk just before drifting off to sleep.

"There," Adam said as he finished with the door. "I hope you intend to call a locksmith first thing in the morning."

"I do." She gestured to the chair opposite hers where his coffee awaited him. "Would you like cream or sugar?"

"No, this is fine," he assured her as he sat and wrapped his hands around the mug. "Are you all right?"

His eyes were filled with such sweet concern that she felt a sudden sting of unexpected tears in her own eyes. She swallowed hard against them. "It's funny, I've seen some horrible things in my time as a cop, things much more horrid than a stuffed bear hanging from a tree. But I have to confess, seeing Mr. Bear hanging from that noose shook me up."

"Of course it did." His soft, deep voice flowed over her like a welcome balm. "These bad things you've seen before…they were never so intimately personal, they were never an implied threat to people you love."

"I just can't help but believe this is intended to harass Rachel and that Michael Rivers is behind it. It's the only thing that makes any sense." She took a sip of her coffee, then continued. "I'm going to go to Sycamore Ridge tomorrow morning and have a little chat with Michael."

"Then I'm going with you."

She looked at him, surprised by the firmness in his statement. "Adam, I can't ask you to do that."

"You didn't ask." He leaned back in the chair, looking perfectly at ease and filled with confidence. "You said your partner is unavailable. I can at least tell by looking at Michael if he resembles the size and shape of the man who slammed me over the head. Besides, I can't let you go confront him alone. I can stand next to you and look menacing."

Despite the seriousness of the events of the night and Breanna's worry, his statement struck her as funny. A burst of laughter escaped her lips. "I'm sorry." She shook her head and drew another deep breath. "You're such a nice man, Adam. I just can't imagine you looking menacing."

The blue of his eyes darkened as his jaw muscles clenched, transforming his features into something hard and dangerous. "If somebody is threatening the people I care about, then I can not only look menacing. I can *be* downright menacing."

Breanna's breath caught somewhere in the center of her chest. He looked so intense...almost dangerous, then he smiled and the threatening danger on his features transformed back to simply deadly handsome.

"You realize you can't do anything to him. In fact you shouldn't even speak to him."

He shrugged. "That's fine. We can let him think I'm your strong, silent, slightly pissed-off partner."

Breanna laughed again, enjoying the release of tension the conversation brought. "All right, then as soon as the locksmith comes and fixes the lock, we'll take off for a drive to Sycamore Ridge."

For a moment they sipped their coffee in silence.

''I like your house,'' he said, breaking the silence before it became too long and uncomfortable. ''Your decorating is so warm and inviting.''

A flush of pleasure swept over her at his words. ''Thank you. I wanted to make it nice, but it was also important to me that I make it a home for Maggie. I didn't want her raised in an apartment and I managed to make a nice arrangement with the landlord.'' She looked at him curiously. ''You mentioned that you were raised by an aunt and uncle. Did they have children of their own?''

''A son.'' He shifted positions and took another sip of his coffee.

''That must have been difficult, at eleven years old trying to become part of a family.''

''They were good people...still are. The first couple of years were a little rocky. I missed my own home, my room...my parents.''

She tried to imagine what that would be like...to be eleven years old and have everything you know and love ripped away from you. She'd been so lucky to have the support, the love of her family both throughout her childhood and now. ''And were you easy to raise or tough?''

''Easy,'' he said without hesitation. He frowned, a touch of pain darkening his eyes. ''As good and loving as my aunt and uncle were, I worried that if I gave them any trouble or heartache, they'd send me away.'' His frown melted away as his lips curved up in one of his sexy grins. ''I know now that it was a totally irrational fear, but it was one my cousin liked to play on.''

''That doesn't sound nice,'' she observed.

He shrugged. ''That's enough about me,'' he replied. "I heard in town that there's some kind of a powwow next weekend at the Cultural Center. Are you involved in that?"

"Minimally, in that I will be there. Actually Maggie is part of the ceremony. She'll be one of the shell-shaker girls on Sunday." She smiled at Adam's bewilderment. "The traditional dance of the Cherokee is the Stomp Dance. There is a leader, assistants and a couple of shell-shaker girls. The girls wear leg rattles made out of turtle shells filled with pebbles."

"Sounds fascinating," he replied. He leaned forward, bringing with him his wonderful scent. "And were you once a shell-shaker?"

She smiled. "Both Savannah and I were shell-shakers."

"And what about Clay? Did he have a role in the ceremonies?"

Her smile faded as she thought of her brother. As much as she loved him and as supportive as he'd always been, she didn't feel like she really knew him. "When he was young he took part in the ceremonies and events, but when he was a teenager he refused to do anything that spoke to his Cherokee blood."

"Why?"

Breanna laced her fingers around her mug. "We aren't sure why. It's been a great source of pain for my mother and I think it's a source of torment for Clay, but it's something he won't talk about."

"When your mother arrived this evening, she said something curious…about a raven?"

"Raven Mocker." As she told him the legend about the most dreaded of all the Cherokee witches, who robbed the dying of their life, she couldn't help but notice that his curly dark hair looked like it would be soft and silky to the touch.

She fought the impulse to reach out and tangle her fingers in his hair, pull his lips to hers and enjoy the excitement, the splendor of a first kiss.

"I've kept you way too long," she said and stood. "It's getting really late." She suddenly needed to be away from him, was afraid that tonight she was too vulnerable, felt too alone.

To her relief, he stood as well and together they walked to the front door. He opened the door and stepped out on the porch. She joined him there, her gaze automatically going to the big tree now devoid of strange fruit.

"Are you sure you're going to be okay?"

"Sure. I'm a single parent and a cop. I'm strong and capable."

He placed two fingers beneath her chin, forcing her to look up at him. "I know all that," he said softly. His eyes were silvery from the illumination of the nearby streetlamp as he gazed at her intently.

In that instant she knew he was going to kiss her. She knew it was foolish to allow it, knew it was a complication she didn't need in her life. However, even knowing all this, she leaned forward, lips slightly parted to accept what he offered.

Tentatively at first, his lips touched hers, almost reverent with whisper softness. It wasn't enough. She wanted more. She reached up and did what she'd thought about doing earlier...tangled her fingers in his silky hair.

His arms wrapped around her and pulled her closer as his kiss became more confident. Masterfully, his mouth plied hers with heat as he pressed her more intimately against the length of his body.

The sensation of his strong, warm body holding her tight, and the cool night air surrounding them was erotic and as his tongue touched hers a ball of heat burst into flames in the pit of Breanna's stomach.

His tongue swirled with hers as his hands moved up and down her back. As his hands cupped her buttocks and pressed her into him, she felt that he was fully aroused. Her knees weakened and her entire body felt like it was nothing more than liquid fire.

It was as if foreplay had begun the moment they met and now a single, first kiss had exploded into a well of desire that threatened to consume her.

His mouth left hers and trailed down her neck. She dropped her head back to allow him better access to the hollows of her throat, the sensitive skin beneath her ears. Each nip and teasing touch of his lips spun her desire higher...deeper.

She wanted him. It was as simple as that. She wanted him in her bed, holding her, making love to her. She trusted him, this man who had appeared out of nowhere. A man who had taken a brick in the head for her protection, who, when he looked at her, reminded her that she wasn't just a single parent and a cop, but a woman as well.

It was obvious he wanted her, too. Pressed so intimately against her, it was impossible to ignore his desire. His lips captured hers once again, this time hot and hungry.

In the back of Breanna's mind was the knowledge that the house was empty. If he came inside and stayed the night, nobody would know. Rachel was gone…Maggie wasn't home. This single night could be theirs.

"Adam," she gasped breathlessly as the kiss ended. "Come back inside with me." She leaned back to look at his face and what she saw in his eyes only confirmed that he wanted her as much as she wanted him. "Come inside and spend the night. Make love to me."

He seemed to stop breathing as his hungry eyes searched her face. He stepped back from her and drew a deep breath of the cool night air. "Breanna, there is nothing I'd rather do at the moment than come inside and spend the night with you."

He dropped his arms from around her and stepped back. Immediately Breanna felt bereaved, as if his embrace had been giving her the very air she breathed and now she was lacking in oxygen.

"But I don't want to make love to you on a night when you've had a shock and might not be making the decision under the best of circumstances." He leaned forward and brushed her lips with his, then stepped back, regret darkening his features. "Believe me, Breanna, if I was certain I wasn't taking advantage of you, I'd be in your bed in a heartbeat."

If she'd wanted him before, his words merely increased her desire for him. But she knew he was right, and a wave of embarrassment swept through her as she realized how forward she had been. "You're right," she said, looking away from him. "I'm not myself and I'm not thinking as clearly as possible."

Again he placed fingers beneath her chin and forced her gaze to his. "I don't know about you, but the moment I met you I was attracted to you. But I don't want us to make a mistake in the heat of a moment when you aren't yourself and thinking clearly." His blue eyes were so earnest, so filled with caring, she found it impossible to maintain any embarrassment.

Although she believed she'd wanted to make love to him, there was a part of her that was grateful he'd called a halt to the prospect. She had ridden an emotional roller coaster from the moment she'd seen Mr. Bear hanging from the tree. She wasn't sure that wasn't playing into her desire for him to stay the night.

"We're still on for tomorrow," he said and dropped his hand from her face. "Going to Sycamore Ridge and finding Michael Rivers."

She nodded. "As soon as the locksmith gets finished."

He leaned forward and kissed her gently on the cheek. "Then I'll see you tomorrow." With those words, he turned and left her porch.

She watched until he disappeared into his house, then she went back inside and carefully locked the door. Once again the silence of the house pressed in around her as she walked up the stairs to her bedroom.

The house was silent, but her head was filled with chaotic noise, the sound of confusing thoughts banging against one another.

As she undressed, she tried to make sense of her thoughts. There was no denying she was vastly attracted to Adam Spencer. From the moment she'd encountered him in her driveway in the middle of the night, she'd felt drawn to him.

She'd felt the exact same way when she'd first met Kurt, although not quite as intense as with Adam. And, like Adam, she'd thought Kurt was a nice guy, a man of moral fiber, a man who could be depended on through thick and thin.

She'd been horribly wrong about Kurt, and how did she know she wasn't horribly wrong about Adam? She had told herself she would never again get her heart involved with a man, she had promised herself she would never subject Maggie to a stepfather.

He wasn't offering a lifetime commitment, a little voice whispered in her head. It was one night of desire shared, one night of passion spent. What was wrong in allowing herself that much?

She got into her nightshirt and got into bed. Closing her eyes she replayed those moments spent in Adam's arms, with his lips so hot and hungry against her own. It had been so long since she'd allowed herself to remember that she was a woman with a woman's needs. Adam had made her remember.

She stretched against the sheets, exhaustion weighing heavy now that her hormones had settled down. She closed her eyes and had almost drifted off to sleep when the telephone rang.

Chapter 7

Walking away from a warm, willing Breanna was the most difficult thing Adam had ever done in his life. But he knew he couldn't make love to her without her knowing the truth about him. And the truth was he was the cousin of a man she hated.

He entered the cottage and sank down on the sofa, waiting for the blood to stop pulsating in his veins, for his heartbeat to return to a more normal pace.

Deciding he was better off pacing than sitting, he stood and began to move back and forth across the tiny living room floor.

He couldn't remember the last time he'd wanted a woman as badly as he wanted Breanna. Kissing her, holding her in his arms had only managed to flame the fires of desire higher and even now he wanted nothing more than to complete what they had begun...to make love to her.

What had Kurt told her about his family? Had he

mentioned who his parents were…that he had a cousin who'd been raised with him like his brother? Adam knew Kurt often rearranged the reality of his family to suit his personal interests.

It didn't matter what Kurt had told Breanna. Adam had to tell her the truth. The longer he put it off, the angrier she would be when he finally did tell her.

Although he had no intention of forming any lasting relationship with her, he wasn't the kind of man to sleep with her under false pretenses. Once he told her the truth, he'd probably never have a chance to make love to her. But he'd rather never have the opportunity to be with her than to be with her with a secret between them.

He flopped on the sofa and raked a hand through his hair in frustration. There were times he wished he could be more like his cousin, times he wished he could take his pleasure as he pleased and never suffer consequences or a pang of guilt. But he couldn't. It simply wasn't in his makeup.

He got up from the sofa and went into the bedroom. He needed to stop thinking and just go to sleep. Tomorrow he would tell Breanna the truth and face whatever consequences came.

It didn't take him long to fall asleep and his dreams were filled with visions of Breanna. In those dreams he was in her bed and her naked skin was pressed against his. Her scent had eddied in the air, driving him half-insane.

They'd made love with a feverish need, a wild abandon, and he awakened with the taste of her lips on his, the scent of her filling his head and the memory of his erotic dreams as vivid and fresh as if they were reality.

It was just after six and the sun was just peeking above the horizon. He grabbed a cup of fresh-brewed coffee and sat outside on his front porch, trying to forget the dreams of the night before.

It was hard to believe that it was just the night before that he and Breanna and Maggie had gone for ice cream. If somebody had told him a month ago that he would take a woman and her child out for an ice-cream cone and he'd enjoy it, he would have laughed in their face.

But he had enjoyed it. Watching Maggie maneuver a double dip of chocolate marshmallow ice cream had been a delight.

As she'd licked and savored the frozen treat, she'd shared little bits of herself with Adam. Her favorite color was pink, but she loved purple as well. Her favorite food was chicken nuggets and, of course, ice cream.

As she chatted, it was obvious that despite her young age she was already well educated in the ways of the Cherokee. She told him about a Cherokee marble game called *Di-ga-da-yo-s-di,* which was played on a field and used marbles the size of billiard balls.

Watching Breanna eat her ice cream was a delight of another kind. With each lick of her tongue on the cone, Adam had felt his blood pressure rise just a little bit more.

He stood and went back into the kitchen for a second cup of coffee, trying to shove sensual thoughts of Breanna from his mind.

He returned to the porch and was still seated there sipping coffee when a panel truck with the words Lock, Stock and Barrel pulled up in front of Breanna's house.

A thin, gangly young man got out of the driver side and loped to Breanna's front door. He was invited inside and returned to his van a few minutes later. Armed with a toolbox, he went back inside.

Adam stood and stretched, working out the kinks that had appeared while he'd sat. It wouldn't take long for an expert to change out the broken lock on Breanna's back door and when the locksmith was finished, Adam knew she'd be ready to make the drive to Sycamore Ridge.

A half an hour later the locksmith pulled away and Adam walked over and knocked on Breanna's door. When she opened the door, concern instantly washed over him.

She looked exhausted, with shadows beneath her eyes and her features taut and drawn. "Good morning," she said with what appeared to be a forced smile.

"What's wrong?" he asked as he followed her through the living room and into the kitchen.

"Coffee?" She gestured him to the table.

He nodded in distraction. "Breanna, has something happened?"

She poured two cups of coffee, then joined him at the table. "I got another phone call last night."

"The same as before? The lullaby?"

She nodded and wrapped her hands around her mug, as if seeking some kind of warmth. "Only, when the song finished playing, a man's voice asked me if I liked the presents he'd left for me."

"You didn't recognize the voice?"

She shook her head. "It sounded raspy and muffled, like he was trying to disguise it."

"Is that all he said?"

"That's it. He hung up before I could say anything."

Adam frowned thoughtfully. "I'm assuming you don't have caller ID."

A faint smile curved her lips. "I don't have cable television or caller ID or an answering machine. My father teases me about being stubborn when it comes to welcoming technology into my home."

"You can't afford to be stubborn right now," Adam observed. "While we're out today we'll get you a caller ID box."

"But can't people do something to block their numbers from showing up on those things?"

"Sure, but I'm hoping this nutcase isn't firing on all cylinders and will make a call without blocking the number."

"I guess it's worth a try," she agreed, then looked at her watch. "It's about an hour's drive to Sycamore Ridge. I guess we could go ahead and take off."

"Fine with me," Adam agreed. He finished his coffee and stood. "Are you sure you're up to it?"

She smiled again, this time fully. "I will be. In the best of times I'm not a morning person. I don't really fully wake up until about ten."

"Then I think it's best if I drive to Sycamore Ridge. I don't want a half-asleep woman behind the wheel of the car when I'm a passenger."

"It's a deal. Just let me get my purse and I'm ready to go."

Minutes later they were in Adam's car headed away from Cherokee Corners. The scent of her perfume filled the small confines of the car and he found himself drawing deep breaths to savor the attractive smell.

In spite of the dark smudges beneath her eyes that indicated a lack of sleep the night before, she grew more animated with each mile that passed.

Adam realized it was going to be difficult keeping things light and easy between them when all he wanted to do was touch her warm skin once again, taste the sweet honey of her mouth.

"Maggie called me first thing this morning and told me that Grandma and Grandpa were fighting over what to have for breakfast. Apparently my mother had already thrown the frying pan at my father."

Adam glanced at her in surprise. "And that doesn't upset you...upset Maggie?"

"My parents' battles are legendary in Cherokee Corners. Maggie knows they fuss and fight and that's just the way they are. By the time she hung up the phone Mom was using the skillet to fry up bacon and eggs."

"I never heard my aunt and uncle exchange a cross word with one another," he said. Although he couldn't count the times he'd heard his aunt cry and his uncle curse over Kurt's antics.

"Different strokes for different folks," she replied. "Some people like the stimulation of good-natured arguments and fighting. Personally, I'd prefer a relationship more like your aunt and uncle's...if I was looking for a relationship, which I'm not."

"Why not?" he asked and cast her another curious glance. "I mean, you're young and beautiful and I'm sure there are lots of men in Cherokee Corners who would like to have a relationship with you." As these words left his lips, he felt a pang of jealousy as he thought of her with any man other than himself.

"I tried the relationship thing once and found it distinctly unpleasant."

"But that doesn't mean another relationship would be unpleasant," he protested.

"Logically, I know that," she agreed softly. She stared out the passenger window for a long moment, then continued. "The idea of doing the dating game is repugnant to me, especially as long as Maggie is so young. I don't want her to be a kid that has 'uncles' drifting in and out of her life."

She turned back to look at him, her dark eyes hinting at inner pain. "Even though logically, I know not all men are like Kurt, I gave him my heart and my trust and he betrayed me. It's hard to trust again, to put your heart on the line and be vulnerable." She cocked her head and eyed him curiously. "So what's your story? You've said you have no plans for a wife or children. Did your heart get kicked by a hard-hearted woman?"

"No, nothing like that." He frowned, trying to figure out how to reply to her, trying to look deep within himself to find the answer. "I don't know, I guess I haven't had much time for any kind of a real relationship. My aunt and uncle loaned me the money to start up my accounting firm and my focus for the past several years has been on that. I finally managed to pay them back last year."

"But that doesn't answer why you don't want a wife and kids." She grinned teasingly. "You're young and handsome. I'm sure there are lots of women who would want a relationship with you."

He laughed. "Maybe there'd be women chasing me down if I was a little more exciting. Women seem to like bad boys. I'm an accountant, for crying out loud.''

She laughed as well, her gaze warm on him. ''I think bad boys have been greatly overrated.''

''Definitely,'' he agreed and once again focused his attention on the road.

How could he begin to explain that he'd decided long ago never to have children who could break his heart, dash his dreams, destroy his hopes for them?

How could he explain to her that there had never been time for women of his own, that in the hours he wasn't at his office or sleeping, he was dealing with Kurt's messes. Bailing him out of jail, helping him pay legal fees, hiding him from jealous husbands, Adam had had no chance to have a life of his own, he was too busy trying to keep Kurt out of trouble.

So what was stopping him now? He had no answer and was somehow grateful when they pulled into the city limits of the tiny town of Sycamore Ridge, forcing him to concentrate on directions to Michael Rivers's apartment rather than the deep-seated reasons he refused to get a life—a woman—of his own.

Adrenaline raced through Breanna as Adam parked down the street from Michael Rivers's apartment building. Sycamore Ridge was a dusty, depressed town. Half of the stores on Main Street were boarded up, their facades weathered to the color of the dust that blew in the air.

The apartment building where Michael lived was a depressing row of flat-roofed living establishments. Trash littered the front, flowing out of metal trash cans that sat near the cracked sidewalk.

Breanna made a courtesy call on her cell phone to

Michael's parole officer, letting him know she intended to question Michael about some threatening phone calls. The parole officer let her know it was his day off and it was fine with him as long as he didn't have to be there.

"Now remember, you can't say or do anything. You just leave it to me," Breanna said to Adam as they got out of the car. She reached for the navy blazer she'd brought with her and put it on over her jeans and white blouse. She pulled her gun from her purse and tucked it into the blazer pocket.

"Are you expecting trouble?" Adam asked, worry lines creasing his forehead.

"No, but I know better than to go into an unknown situation unprepared." She smiled. "Don't look so worried. This is just routine stuff."

However, as she and Adam approached apartment 3D, Breanna knew this was anything but routine. She was an off-duty cop taking a civilian with her to question an ex-con without her boss's permission.

She knew the crime wasn't big enough to warrant this, but she'd be damned if she'd allow Michael Rivers to cause Rachel and herself another day of fear.

She was intensely aware of Adam next to her and she shot a surreptitious glance his way and saw that his jaw was clenched tight and his eyes were narrowed as if in anticipation of trouble. She had a feeling that despite his easygoing, good guy appearance, Adam was a man who could handle anything that came his way. He made her feel protected despite the fact that she was the one who had a gun in her pocket.

The door to apartment 3D had once been a burgundy color, but age and abuse had turned it into the brownish red of old blood. Breanna knocked briskly as tension ripped through her.

Michael would know her on sight. She had been instrumental in his arrest for the assault on Rachel. She'd testified at his trial. He would not be happy to see her again.

There was no answer to her knock. "Maybe he isn't home," Adam said.

"He's probably still in bed. His P.O. said he works the evening shift at a convenience store." She knocked once again more forcefully.

"Hang on," a disgruntled deep voice yelled from inside. A moment passed then the door flew open. Michael Rivers stood in the doorway, clad only in a pair of jeans he'd obviously hastily pulled on. His dark eyes narrowed as he saw Breanna.

"Hello, Michael," Breanna said. He was just as she'd remembered him, except on the day he'd been sentenced he'd had shoulder-length dark hair. Now, his head was shaved. A tattoo of a skull and cross-bones decorated his upper left arm.

"What the hell do you want?" He glanced behind him, then stepped half-out of the doorway, the door held firmly in his hand.

"I just want to talk to you for a minute or two."

Michael's gaze shot to Adam. "And who the hell are you?"

"If I wanted you to know my name, I would have introduced myself," Adam said, his voice hard as Michael's gaze.

Michael snorted. "Cops…they got all the answers. So what the hell you bothering me for?"

"You been visiting Cherokee Corners? Maybe having some phone contact with Rachel?'' Breanna asked.

He raised his eyebrows. ''You think I'm stupid? If I go to Cherokee Corners, it's a violation of the condition of my parole and as far as getting in touch with Rachel...'' He snorted again. ''Not interested. I got me a new life and a new woman.'' He opened the door and looked back inside. ''Hey, Alison, get out here.''

A young, hard-looking blonde appeared in the doorway. Michael slung an arm around her slender shoulder and pulled her tightly, possessively against him. ''This is Alison. We're gonna get married in a couple of months...once I'm on my feet. I don't need to talk to Rachel and I never want to step a foot into Cherokee Corners again.''

''Where were you last night between the hours of seven and midnight?'' Breanna asked. There was a sinking feeling deep in her heart, in her soul.

''At work. Check it out, lady cop. I worked from 5:00 p.m. until after one. If you're trying to pin something on me, you're out of gas.''

''I will check it out,'' Breanna said coolly. ''But if I find you're causing problems for Rachel or if I see the end of your nose in Cherokee Corners, I'll have you back behind bars so fast it will take two weeks for your tattoo to find you.''

''You done hassling me?'' he asked arrogantly.

''For now,'' she replied.

''But that doesn't mean we won't be back,'' Adam added.

Without another word, Michael pulled his girl-friend back into the apartment and slammed the door shut.

"Pleasant fellow," Adam said as they walked back to his car.

"Yeah, I guess Rachel proves your point about women having a weakness for bad boys…only in Michael's case there were no redeeming qualities whatsoever." She tried not to show her distress as she played and replayed in her mind every nuance of her conversation with Michael Rivers.

She slid into the passenger seat as Adam got in the driver's side. He started the engine, then turned to look at her. "I'm assuming you want to check out the convenience store where that punk works."

She smiled at him. "Keep this up, ace, and you'll be an excellent candidate for the police academy."

"Thanks, but I think I'll keep my day job."

"You wouldn't want to be a cop anyway. The hours are awful and the pay stinks. Besides, one day you'll paint a picture that will earn you great riches and respect in the art community."

"So where's this convenience store?" he asked abruptly.

"It should be just ahead on the left," she replied, her thoughts going back to the conversation with Michael. As much as she wanted to believe he was lying, that it had been him who had made the phone calls and hung the things in her tree, her gut instinct told her Michael had told her the truth.

"You know, I'm pretty sure Michael wasn't the man peeking into your windows," Adam said. "The man I saw was taller…bigger. Is it possible the window-peeper has nothing to do with the calls? Maybe some horny teenager or just your ordinary creep?"

"I guess it's possible," she said. "But a horny

teenager or an ordinary creep wouldn't have been so quick to hit you upside the head with a brick. Whoever it was, he could have killed you.''

Adam pulled into the convenience store parking lot. ''It looks like we're the only customers,'' he said. ''Maybe I'll help the local economy and buy a soda. Want one?''

''Why not?'' They got out of the car and walked into the gas station quick stop. Adam went directly to the coolers in the back while Breanna asked the kid behind the counter if a manager was in.

''Hey, Joe...somebody out here wants to talk to you,'' the kid yelled.

A big man, belly hanging over an ornate turquoise belt, lumbered out from the back room. He offered Breanna a big smile until she flashed her badge, then his smile fell and he emitted a long-suffering sigh. ''Yeah, what can I do for you, Officer?''

''Michael Rivers...did he work for you last night?''

''Yeah, he was here. Worked from about five until after one.''

''Were you here as well?'' Breanna asked as Adam joined her at the counter, two soft drink cans in his hands.

''What's the point of having help if I got to be here all the time with them?''

''Then, how do you know he was here?'' Breanna countered.

He pointed a pudgy finger to a camera in the ceiling. ''Every night I load a tape and every morning I watch it. You'd be surprised how some of the hired help will try to rob you blind.''

''You had problems with Rivers?'' she asked.

"Nah. He shows up on time and stays late if necessary and so far he seems honest enough." He scratched his belly. "Sodas are on the house," he said to Adam, then looked back at Breanna. "Anything else I can do for you?"

"You have a copy of this past week's schedule for Michael?" she asked.

"Hang on, I can get you one." He disappeared into the back and returned a moment later with a sheet of paper.

"We appreciate your help," Breanna said and she and Adam left the store.

The minute they were back in the car and on the road to Cherokee Corners, Breanna stared at the copy of the work schedule for the convenience store. A knot of apprehension twisted in the pit of her stomach.

"According to this, on the nights and at the times I got those phone calls, Michael was at work."

"Is it possible he might have called from work?" Adam asked. She could tell by the tone of his voice that he was thinking the same thing she was...if it wasn't Michael Rivers tormenting Rachel, then was it possible it was somebody trying to torment *her?*

Chapter 8

The drive from Sycamore Ridge back to Cherokee Corners was accomplished in relative silence. Adam felt Breanna's worry wafting from her, but he had no soothing platitudes to offer her.

"It's after eleven," he said as they entered the city limits. "How about we grab some lunch out, then we can pick up that caller ID box for you."

"That sounds good," she agreed.

"You need to direct me to the best place in town for lunch."

"I'm assuming you're talking about someplace between a drive-up window and coat and tie required."

He smiled at her. "You're reading my mind." He was glad to see her return his smile, her features less tense than they'd been moments before.

"Red Rock Café on the city square has a really nice lunch buffet," she offered.

"Then Red Rock Café it is," he agreed.

Twenty minutes later they faced each other across a table, plates heaped high in front of them. "I always eat too much when I come here." She looked at her plate as if she had no idea how all that food had gotten on it.

"I'm obviously no slouch when it comes to the 'my eyes are probably bigger than my stomach' department," he replied and gestured to his overfilled plate.

As they began to eat, it was as if they'd made an unspoken pact not to discuss anything unpleasant.

They talked of the books they had read, surprised to discover they both shared a voracious appetite for mysteries. She shared with him some of the Cherokee legends and they discussed the tragic history of the Trail of Tears.

Adam loved watching her as she talked, her features animated and her eyes shining. He envied her her strong sense of identity, the pride she took in belonging to a group of people who saw themselves as caretakers of the earth.

They lingered over coffee and he wondered if she was as reluctant as he was to walk out of the restaurant and back into the complications of life.

"Thank you," she said as they left the restaurant.

"For what? You insisted we go dutch."

"Thank you for letting me ramble on about nothing to keep me from thinking about everything."

"It was purely selfish on my part," he assured her. "I enjoy listening to you."

Her gaze was soft and warm. "You're a nice man, Adam Spencer."

He wasn't a nice man, he thought a few minutes

later as he watched her talking to a salesman in the phone department of a discount chain store.

He wasn't a nice man at all. As she listened to the salesman going over the features of the various caller ID products, Adam wondered when he would have the chance to kiss her lush lips again.

As she was paying for the machine they hoped would lead to the man making the phone calls...the man who had hung poor Mr. Bear by a noose, Adam wondered what it would be like to make love to her, to caress every inch of her body until she writhed with want...with need.

Despite her quietness on the way home, he'd been intensely aware of her in the small confines of the car. Her fragrance, the combination of clean mingling with the evocative scent she wore filled the car. It had been impossible for him not to have been affected by it.

"Want some help connecting this?" he asked as they pulled into his driveway.

"If you don't mind. I've already confessed to you that I'm technology-challenged."

He didn't tell her that connecting it was simple. They got out of the car and went into her house. He carried the sack with the caller identification machine. "The first thing you need to decide is what phone jack you want it hooked up to."

She frowned thoughtfully as she took off her blazer and laid it across the back of the sofa. "Both times he's called it's been late...minutes after I've gone to bed. Maybe we should put it on the phone jack in my bedroom."

Adam thought of the bedroom he'd seen the night

before, the rumpled bed sheets that had momentarily filled his head with hot visions of lovemaking.

He steeled himself for the sensual barrage of entering the intimacy of the room where she slept... where she dreamed.

"Excuse the mess," she said as she entered the room ahead of him and hastily pulled up the bedspread. "After years of being told to make my bed, my secret rebellion is that once I left my parents' home, I stopped."

"Don't apologize," he replied. "I don't care what your bedroom looks like." Which of course wasn't true. He found everything about the room fascinating and wondered what secrets about her he could glean by looking around. The walls were a light beige and held an array of paintings he guessed were by the woman she'd told him about. A large, intricate dreamcatcher hung on the wall over her bed.

Although the bed was unmade, the rest of the room was in impeccable order. The only item on the dresser was a wooden jewelry box neatly centered on a sky-blue scarf, letting him know she was a woman who didn't like clutter.

She slept on the left side of the bed. The nightstand on that side held a small reading lamp, a copy of a newly released mystery paperback, the telephone and a clock radio. The nightstand on the other side of the bed held a stunning array of silk flowers in an earthen vase.

"Adam?"

"Oh...sorry." He realized she was waiting for him to get to work. He sat on the edge of her bed to pull the caller ID from its carton, his fingers feeling clumsy and awkward.

Here, amid the covers where she slept, the scent of her seemed to waft in the air with enough potency to seep into his very pores.

"Is there anything I can do?" she asked.

"Just stay out of my way," he said more brusquely than he'd intended. If she came too close he was afraid he might grab her and tumble with her to the bed to finish what they had begun last night.

He was both grateful and disappointed that she did as he bid, moving across the room to lean with her back against the dresser.

He finally managed to get the caller ID box out of its carton and quickly plugged it into the wall jack and the phone into the back of the box. "That's it," he said.

She eyed him dubiously. "Are you sure? That seemed terribly easy."

"Actually, it was all very difficult. Only a man of my expertise and intelligence could have done it and made it look easy." He strove desperately for a lightness of tone to stymie the rising tide of desire that threatened. "I hope you're quite impressed."

"Oh, I am." She pushed off from the dresser and walked toward him. The look in her eyes, her loose-hipped saunter as she approached where he stood at the side of the bed made his heartbeat quicken.

She stopped when she stood no more than an inch away from him. "Thank you, Adam. Thank you for hooking up my caller ID box and for going with me to Sycamore Ridge." She leaned into him and he was lost.

Despite every intention he had to the contrary, his arms wound around her and pulled her tight against him. It was impossible not to kiss her eagerly parted lips, impossible not to fall head-first into a vortex of desire too powerful to avoid.

Her heart beat with the rhythm of his own... fast...frantic. They tumbled on the bed and Adam had the sensation of drowning, as if he were utterly powerless against the waves of passion that pounded him.

Her mouth was hungry against his as her hands moved up beneath his shirt to caress the bare skin of his back. It was as if fire resided in the tips of her fingers and Adam was lost in the flames.

He moved his hands down her back until he got to the bottom of her blouse, then back up again inside her blouse. Her skin was velvety soft and a moan ripped itself loose from deep in his throat.

The kiss, that seemed to last not long enough, ended as she pulled slightly away from him and began unbuttoning her blouse.

Someplace in the dark recesses of his mind a small voice whispered a warning, but at that moment her blouse fell open and the sight of her perfect breasts clad only in a pale pink lace bra stifled the tiny voice.

Moments later she was in his arms once again, this time her blouse and lacy bra on the floor next to his shirt. His hand cupped one of her breasts, his thumb raking over her turgid nipple.

His mouth kissed down her jawline, lingered in the sweet hollow of her throat, then moved to capture one of her nipples.

She gasped and her fingernails bit into his back. He teased her with his tongue, laving first one then the other breast.

He pressed his hips against hers and she arched up

to meet him, the friction of her jeans against his half stimulating and half tormenting.

It wasn't until her fingers touched the top button at the waistband of his jeans that he suffered a single moment of clear, rational thought.

He grabbed her hand and groaned, not moving a muscle for a long moment. She froze as well. The room was silent except for their rapid, openmouthed breathing. ''Adam?'' she finally said.

How he didn't want to halt what had been about to happen. How desperately he wished he could make love to her and not worry about any consequence. ''Breanna…we need to talk.''

She looked at him incredulously. ''Now? I mean… it can't wait?'' Apparently the expression on his face answered her question. She moved away from him and reached down to grab her blouse, a frown of worry furrowing her brow.

He didn't answer for a moment, but instead got up from the bed and grabbed his shirt. He pulled it on, then looked at her, trying not to notice that her breasts were fully visible through the sheer white material.

''Adam…what is it?'' she asked.

He averted his gaze and drew a hand heavily across his jaw, wondering how in the hell to tell her who he was and what had brought him to Cherokee Corners. It suddenly struck him that not only did he have to confess who he was, but he was the one who was going to tell her that the man she had married and divorced, the man who was Maggie's father, was dead.

She had no idea what was going on, but dread raked through her as she waited for Adam to talk to her. Her heart still pounded with the memory of his kisses, his sweet touch. Her body still experienced the languid warmth of imminent lovemaking. What could he have to tell her that was so important it had caused him to stop what they had been about to do?

"Why don't we go downstairs," he said, his gaze still not meeting hers.

"All right," she agreed, disquieted by the fact that whatever he had to tell her, he didn't want to do it in her bedroom.

He followed her down the stairs to the living room where she sat anxiously on the edge of the sofa and he remained standing by the fireplace hearth.

She felt oddly disconnected, as if half of her was still upstairs in his arms and the other half was waiting for a shoe to drop soundly on her head. She just couldn't imagine what form the shoe would take.

He rubbed a hand across his lower jaw, a gesture that had become familiar to her in the brief time she'd known him. It indicated deep thought…and stress. She wanted to scream at him to speak, wanted to demand he tell her what was so important it had interrupted their lovemaking.

He drew a deep breath and looked at her, his eyes a dark, slate blue. "Remember I told you that my parents died when I was eleven and I was raised by an aunt and uncle?"

She nodded with bewilderment.

He moved from the fireplace to the opposite side of the sofa and sank down wearily, as if the weight of the world had crashed down onto his shoulders.

"Adam?" She leaned forward and placed a hand on his arm. "What is it? Tell me."

"The people who raised me were Kurt's parents."

For a long moment his words didn't compute. Kurt? Why was he talking about Kurt? When the connection was made, it crashed through her with a thunderous roar. She jerked her hand back from him and jumped to her feet, myriad emotions ripping through her.

Confusion was the emotion most readily identified, but just beneath the surface simmered a stir of anger along with an overwhelming sense of betrayal. "You're Kurt's cousin?"

He nodded and a rolling dread poured through her with a nauseating intensity. "What are you doing here? What do you want? Why in the hell are you here? And why didn't you tell me who you were from the very beginning?"

He jumped at the sharpness in her voice and stood, his hands out as if to appeal to her. "I'm sorry I didn't tell you," he said. He drew another heavy sigh. "I wanted to get to know you and was afraid you wouldn't give me the chance if you knew who I was."

Dropping his hands to his sides, he sat back down and patted the sofa next to him. "Please, Breanna, give me a chance to explain."

She didn't want to hear what he had to say. He'd lied to her, perhaps not outright, but through omission by not telling her immediately of his relationship to Kurt. Knowing now who he was changed everything she'd thought about him, tainted every moment she'd spent with him. "You haven't told me why you're here," she said. She didn't move from her standing position, refused to sit next to a man whose actions were now all in question.

"I'm here because I promised Kurt I'd look in on

you and Maggie and make sure you both were all right.'' His gaze seemed to caress her and in their depths she saw a sadness she didn't understand. ''I made the promise to Kurt moments before he died.''

The shock of his words forced her to sink back down on the edge of the sofa. ''Before he died?'' she echoed the words faintly.

''Two weeks ago Kurt died from injuries he sustained in a motorcycle accident.''

He fell silent, as if to allow his words to sink in. Dead. Kurt was dead. How was that possible? She'd always somehow believed that Kurt was the kind of man who ran too fast through life for death to ever catch up with him.

She was surprised to feel a sudden sting of tears as she thought of the man she had married and divorced.

A well of grief swept through her, not for herself, but for Maggie, who would now never have the opportunity to have any kind of a relationship with her father.

It was also grief for Kurt. Even though he had walked out on her and told her he didn't care about having a relationship with his child, someplace deep in Breanna's heart she'd hoped he'd change his mind, but death had stolen that possibility away.

He'd missed out on knowing the wonder and delight of his daughter. She drew a deep breath and quickly swiped at the tears that had fallen.

''His last wish was that I come out here to Cherokee Corners and check on you and Maggie,'' Adam continued.

She embraced a new anger as she gazed at him. ''Fine. You're here. You've checked. And as you can see we're both just fine.'' Her sense of betrayal

emerged as she stood once again. She'd trusted him
and once again she realized her trust in a man had
been sadly misplaced. Bitterness ripped through her.
"Tell me something, Adam. Was it the way you and
Kurt were raised that made you both want to bed a
half-breed?"

He gasped and his eyes widened in shock. He
jumped up from the sofa. "Don't talk that way," he
exclaimed.

"Why not? That's the way your cousin spoke to
me." She stopped herself from going back to that
time, back to the hurtful things Kurt had said to her.
She didn't want to go back there. "Just go, Adam,"
she said wearily. "You've done what you promised
Kurt you would do. Your mission is complete."

"Not exactly," he said, not moving from his position. "There's the matter of Kurt's parents. Aunt
Anita and Uncle Edward don't know about Maggie
yet, but I'm sure..."

Breanna held up a hand to stop him. "Anita and
Edward? Anita and Edward Randolf are Kurt's parents?"

He nodded and once again shock ripped through
her. She knew who Anita and Edward Randolf
were...she'd read articles about the dynamic million-
aire and his wife. They were high-society, benefactors
of the arts and a variety of charities in Kansas City.

"Kurt told me his parents were dead," she said
numbly. He'd told her a lot of things about his parents, none of it good. "He told me they died in a car
accident the year before I met him." God help her,
she didn't know what to believe about anything and
anyone...especially Adam Spencer.

"They're alive and grieving the passing of their

only son. Knowing about Maggie would help ease some of their pain.''

Breanna felt as if she'd been cast into a dark, fathomless sea where nothing was familiar and as it should be. Kurt was dead…his parents were alive… Adam was his cousin and now each and every one of Adam's actions since she'd met him took on new meaning.

Again she reached for the anger as she thought of Adam's kisses…his caresses. He'd made her think he cared about her, but he'd obviously had ulterior motives. He didn't want her. He wanted Maggie for his grieving aunt and uncle. And everything she knew about the Randolfs frightened her.

''I don't want you telling them about Maggie. Maggie and I are doing just fine. We don't need them in our lives….'' Her heart hardened with anger…with fear.

''Breanna…'' he protested.

''And I want you out of here now.'' She walked to the front door and opened it. ''Get out, Adam. We have nothing more to say to each other.''

He stood, obviously reluctantly. ''I have a lot more to say,'' he countered. ''I need you to know that I regret not telling you the truth the night that I met you in your driveway. I need you to know that no matter what you're thinking now, I didn't mean to hurt you. That's why I couldn't make love to you…not without you knowing the truth.''

''Gee, I'm glad you cleared it all up. Thanks,'' she said coolly. ''And now, get out.''

He advanced toward the door and she stepped aside to allow him to pass. She didn't look at him, found that it hurt too much.

He stopped directly in front of her and she knew he wanted her to look at him, wanted her to see the appeal in his eyes. Exhaustion overwhelmed her... sheer mental exhaustion. "Please..." she said softly without raising her gaze from the floor. "Please... just go."

She held her breath and expelled it only when he walked out the front door. She closed the door after him and leaned on it heavily, tears once again burning hot in her eyes.

Too much...her head ached from trying to wrap around all the information she'd learned. And most of that information had been positively stunning.

She shoved off from the door, locked it, then went back to the sofa and sank down on the cushions. She grabbed a throw pillow and hugged it to her chest, as if the cushioned softness could staunch the ache in her heart.

Kurt was dead. The love she'd once believed she had for him was long gone, banished beneath the weight of broken dreams and unfulfilled promises. But just because she didn't love him anymore didn't mean she didn't grieve over his death.

She'd always held out a tiny modicum of hope that eventually Kurt would grow up and be a man, take responsibility not for her, but for their daughter. The crushing of that hope was painful.

The information that Kurt's parents were not only alive and well, but were the renowned businessman Edward Randolf and his wife, Anita, filled her with fear.

Over the nine months that she had known Kurt, he had occasionally spoken about his parents. He'd told her that they had been people who worshipped their money, who liked to possess things, but had little use for people.

On the day he'd left her, he'd mentioned that it was a good thing his parents were dead because they'd never stand for a half-breed raising their grand-kid.

It was the memory of these words that now stirred a fear deep in her soul. The Randolfs had enough money to get what they wanted and if they decided they wanted Maggie, she had a feeling they'd find a way to get her. This thought was so terrifying, she shoved it away as more tears flowed.

Instead, she thought of Adam, who had come here with a specific purpose in mind and had woven his way into her life under false pretenses.

In just three short days, he'd made her care for him, made her believe that she could trust him as she'd never trusted a man, other than her father, before. She'd trusted him so much she'd been willing…eager to make love with him, share an intimacy she'd guarded intensely since Kurt's defection.

It had all been lies. He was in her life not because he cared about her, but because he'd been doing a duty, fulfilling a promise to a dead man. He was in her life because he wanted to give his grieving aunt and uncle the gift of her daughter.

She swiped at her cheeks, bitterness filling her. Four days ago her life had seemed so uncomplicated. She worked her job, assured that Maggie was well cared for by a loving nanny. On her days off she spent time with her daughter and her family and the biggest worry she had was whether she'd ever be able to get Maggie to try something other than chicken nuggets when they ate out.

She closed her eyes, wishing away the disturbing phone calls, the news that Kurt's parents were alive and most of all, Adam Spencer.

The ringing of the phone awakened her. She grabbed up the receiver next to the sofa and sat up. "Hello?"

"Bree, it's Clay."

"Hi," she said and attempted to shake off her sleep. "What's up?"

"I just wanted you to know that I dusted the cradle thoroughly for prints and it yielded nothing. I would guess that the perp wore gloves."

"Thanks, Clay. I can't say I'm surprised." Although she was bitterly disappointed. It would have been nice had Clay been able to lift prints and the mystery of the phone caller had been solved.

"Are you okay?" he asked after a moment of hesitation. His question surprised her. Clay rarely seemed attuned to feelings or if he was attuned, he rarely asked about other people's emotions.

"I'm all right," she replied. "Why?"

"I don't know...you just sound sort of funny."

"I was napping and your call woke me up."

"Oh, okay. Let me know if there's anything else you need," he said briskly. She could tell his mind had already moved on.

"I will...and thanks, Clay." She hung up the phone and looked at the clock. It was already after five. She must have been asleep for over an hour.

The night stretched out before her...empty...lonely. With Rachel and Maggie gone, the house felt cold and alien. She mentally rebelled at the thought of sleeping in her bedroom, which she knew would now smell of Adam's scent.

She got up and stretched and decided what she really wanted to do was go to her parents' house and spend the night there, in the comfort of the three people who loved her most, her mother, her father and sweet Maggie.

Tomorrow she would deal with her life. Tonight she just wanted the company of her family around her and no thoughts of Adam Spencer to intrude.

Chapter 9

Adam had known telling her the truth would be difficult. He'd known what he had to tell her would be a shock, but he hadn't expected it to be as difficult as it had been.

Even a full day later, the image of her lovely face with her expressive eyes as he'd told her the truth about Kurt, about himself, was permanently emblazoned in his brain. As his words had sunk in, her features had fallen and her eyes had radiated myriad emotions—anger—and pain.

He'd left her and had been angry with himself, his own heart aching in a way he'd never felt before. He'd never meant to hurt her. Dammit, he should have told her who he was and why he was here in Cherokee Corners the moment he'd first met her.

But on that night when they'd first met, the belief that she might be a prostitute had thrown him for a loop. The other thing that had thrown him for a loop was her comment about bedding a half-breed.

It had been ugly and shocking and he couldn't help but wonder if Kurt had left far deeper scars on her than Adam had initially suspected.

He'd watched her drive off and had known instinctively that she wouldn't be back for the remainder of the night. He'd give her a day or two to cool down, then he'd hope to have a rational, nonemotional talk with her. Hopefully he could make her see that Edward and Anita deserved a chance to be a part of Maggie's life. Hopefully he could make her understand that he'd never meant to hurt her in any way.

She came home the next day just before three and by four was getting into her car again. He assumed she was going to work. He was seated on the porch when she left and she gave no indication she saw him there, although he was certain he couldn't be missed.

He decided to walk into town for dinner, not finding much appeal in cooking for himself and eating alone in the shabby little kitchen.

As he walked toward the city square his thoughts turned to Kurt. His love for his cousin had always been unconditional, but as he thought of Breanna's pain and anger when she spoke of him, as he thought of the little fatherless Maggie, he felt the edge of an emotion that was both alien and distinctly uncomfortable.

He focused on the scenery he passed instead. He wasn't ready to evaluate the emotions he now felt when he thought of Kurt.

It was a perfect early May night. The air was cool and scented with sweet-smelling flowers and as he passed people working in their yards or sitting on their porches, they waved with small-town friendliness. Nice, he thought...much nicer than his sterile apartment where he had no idea who his neighbors were or what they did.

He ate at a café on the city square that advertised a stupendous daily special. It was meat loaf. He people-watched while he ate, finding other people's actions and chatter far less disturbing than his own thoughts.

After his meal he walked to the Redbud Bed and Breakfast and into the ice-cream parlor where Alyssa worked. Once again she was behind the counter and she greeted him with a reserved smile as he slid onto a stool at the counter and ordered a cup of coffee.

"So, you're Kurt's cousin," she said as she set the cup and saucer in front of him.

"You must have spoken to Breanna," he said with a grimace as tension rose inside him. "You didn't poison my coffee, did you?"

"No. The way I see it, you can pick your friends, but you can't pick your relatives."

"I guess if we could pick our relatives, nobody would have a crazy Uncle Harry who always ended up with a lampshade on his head at family gatherings," he said wryly.

She smiled and some of his tension dissipated. "In our family it's crazy Uncle Sammy. He's Uncle Thomas's brother and definitely the black sheep and most fun of the family."

He took a sip of his coffee and eyed her curiously. "So you knew my cousin?"

"For the brief time he was here. I'm afraid I didn't think much of him even though Bree was crazy about him. They married after just a month of knowing each other, far too quickly. I knew he was going to break her heart from the moment I met him.'' She eyed him intently, her dark gaze appearing to look deep inside of him. ''And I have a feeling if you aren't careful, you could break her heart as well.''

He laughed, although with little amusement. ''No chance of that. I've been quite clear with Breanna that I want no ties, that I'm not interested in a relationship. Besides, at the moment she isn't even speaking to me.''

Alyssa tilted her head to one side, not taking her gaze from him. ''Then perhaps she'll break your heart.''

He laughed again, distinctly uncomfortable. ''That isn't going to happen, either. Breanna is a loose end in Kurt's life that I needed to tie up. That's all.''

''Loose ends have a way of snarling you all up if you aren't careful,'' she replied.

He took another sip of his coffee, then eyed her curiously. ''Is this one of your visions talking or just idle speculation?''

She frowned. ''The only vision I have at the moment is one where I see that my darling cousin talks too much.''

''She was worried and mentioned to me about your visions. She said you've been having some bad feelings lately.''

Her eyes darkened, but she shrugged. ''It's a curse from my grandmother on my mother's side. She, too, suffered from visions.''

''If you hold my hand, will you be able to see my future?'' he asked, genuinely curious.

She shook her head, obviously not offended by his

question. "It doesn't work that way. I wish it did, but it doesn't."

"Then how does it work?" Although he was intrigued, he also knew in the back of his mind that what he was doing by talking with Alyssa was keeping a connection to Breanna.

"I don't know how it works. Most of the time I get a bit of a headache and I know I'm about to have a vision. The vision itself is kind of like seeing the coming attractions of a movie...a flash of scenes that don't always initially make sense."

"Like what...? Tell me about a vision you've had in the past."

She looked around, as if hoping somebody would need her attention, but the only other people in the place was a young couple sharing a banana split. They were too engrossed in each other to be paying any attention to Adam and Alyssa.

She sighed and looked back at him. "Six months ago I was eating dinner in my apartment and I got a vision. In it, my father was telling me the story of Raven Mocker." She looked at him questioningly.

"The witch who comes to take a life," he said.

She nodded and continued. "Anyway, I couldn't understand why he was telling me a story I'd heard a hundred times before. Then I realized as he spoke that I was cold...colder than I'd ever been in my life. When the vision passed I tried to tell myself it meant nothing, but I decided to try to get in touch with my father."

"And...?" Adam found himself completely caught up in her story.

"And he wasn't home. My mother said she'd been expecting him for the past two hours, but hadn't heard from him and just assumed his last job of the day had been a bigger one than he'd expected. My father works as a heating and refrigeration repairman. When I thought about the cold I'd felt during my vision I was suddenly afraid.''

She paused and grabbed the coffeepot and refilled his cup. When she continued speaking, her eyes were darker than he'd have thought possible. ''I got hold of Dad's boss and insisted he meet me at the location of Dad's last job of the day, a butcher shop. The shop was closed, but we found Dad there. He'd been accidentally locked inside a walk-in freezer. He was suffering frostbite and hypothermia. The doctor said if he'd been in that freezer another hour or so we might have lost him.

''So your visions can sometimes save lives,'' he said.

''Sometimes…if I can figure out what they mean. The torment is in figuring them out too late, in knowing that something horrible is happening or about to happen and not being able to stop it.

''Do you always pass out after a vision?''

''No, only after a particularly bad vision.''

''Is that what happened on the day of the barbecue? You had a bad vision?

He didn't think it was possible for her eyes to grow darker, but they did. ''Yes and no,'' she replied softly.

She broke her eye contact with him and looked around the parlor. He didn't know if she was checking to see if any of the patrons needed anything or if she was merely grounding herself in the here and now.

When she looked back at him her eyes were still as dark as night and filled with what appeared to be fear. ''I'm not sure what happened at the barbecue. It wasn't like my usual visions. It was like death…a feeling of loss, of emptiness too great to bear.''

"What do you think it means?'' Adam asked as a chill walked up his spine.

"I think it means somebody close to me, somebody I love is in grave danger.'' They both jumped as the bell over the front door tinkled and a family of four walked in.

She freshened up his coffee again, then stepped away from him to wait on the newcomers. Adam had a feeling she wouldn't be back to talk to him about her visions, or Breanna or anything else of importance.

He finished his coffee, waved a goodbye and left the ice-cream parlor. As he walked toward the cottage, thoughts of Breanna filled his head.

Perhaps it was a good thing he'd made her angry. He'd been getting too close to her, had been seduced by her beauty and charm, her strength and her wit. Telling her the truth had put distance between them, and that wasn't a bad thing.

If he was smart, he'd get the hell out of Dodge, pack up his things and get back to his own life. He'd done what he'd promised Kurt he would do, he'd found Breanna and Maggie and they were doing just fine. He'd never intended to get caught up in Breanna's life, hadn't anticipated being charmed by her family.

He should return to Kansas City, tell his aunt and uncle about Maggie and let them deal with Breanna to gain some sort of grandparent rights. He could step away now and remain uninvolved in the whole mess, he told himself.

He knew he was lying to himself. Despite all his

protests to the contrary, he was already involved. Perhaps if he had never tasted the sweetness of Breanna's lips, maybe if he'd never held her warm and willing body against his own, he might have been able to convince himself that he wasn't involved.

But he had tasted her mouth and he had caressed her heated body and there was no way he could pretend to himself that he could just walk away and not look back. Especially not with Alyssa's ominous words ringing in his ears.

He halted in front of Breanna's house and stared up at the big oak tree, remembering the shock of seeing the pink plastic cradle and Mr. Bear hanging there. His stomach knotted with anger and a touch of fear.

Again Alyssa's words resounded in his head. "I think it means somebody close to me, somebody I love is in grave danger."

Was it Breanna? Was Alyssa's feeling coming from the same place as the phone calls and implied threat of a hanging stuffed animal?

He entered his cottage, knowing that he wasn't leaving Cherokee Corners, he wasn't going anywhere. There was no way he could leave knowing she might be in danger. He moved to his kitchen window and stared out at her house.

He wasn't going anywhere until he knew they weren't in any danger. If she never spoke to him again, then so be it. He would be a silent sentry watching over her, keeping her and her daughter safe from harm to the best of his ability.

Breanna was having a bad week. She'd arrived at work on Wednesday to discover that drug-trafficking charges against a repeat offender had been dropped that day in court due to a legal technicality. Although she and Abe hadn't been participants in the actual arrest of the creep, they had both logged long hours in surveillance on him.

Every day when she left for work Adam was seated on his porch, and he was there once again when she returned home after work. She was grateful he didn't try to speak to her because she certainly wasn't ready to talk to him. She spoke to Maggie and Rachel every day at her parents' house and was surprised that the strange, lullaby phone calls appeared to have stopped.

She figured one of two things, either the phone calls had truly been made by Michael Rivers and their little visit to him had scared him off, or they had been the result of somebody's idea of a sick joke and the joker had gotten bored and moved on to another game. In either case she was grateful that the disturbing calls had ceased.

By Friday night she was starting to feel a little bit better. She'd made arrangements for both Maggie and Rachel to return home Sunday after the festivities at the Cultural Center. It would be good to have them back where they belonged, good to have their lives back to some semblance of normal.

Her positive thinking lasted until her partner, Abe, delivered the bombshell that he'd be leaving the force for retirement.

They were seated at side-by-side desks in the station house, catching up on paperwork when Abe told her he'd put in his two-weeks' notice.

"You knew this was coming, Bree," Abe said. "I've been telling you for months that retirement for me was right around the corner."

"I know. I just didn't realize the corner was so close." She was beginning to feel as if her life would never be the same again. Kurt was dead, Adam was a liar and betrayer and now her partner was leaving her.

"Ah, don't look so glum," Abe said sympathetically. "You've got a great career ahead of you, Bree. You don't need an old coot like me hanging around your neck." He scowled, his grizzly gray eyebrows nearly meeting in the center of his forehead. "I just wish I was going out on a bang."

"What do you mean?"

"I dunno. I wish we were breaking a major prostitution ring or putting the finishing touches on a multimillion-dollar drug bust. I hate to think that the last job I'll ever do as a cop is arrest some hapless John with his pants half-down."

Breanna grinned at him. "One John at a time, that's how we clean up the streets of our fair city." She noticed a blond hair shining on the collar of his dark jacket. She leaned over and plucked it off. "Have you got some sexy blonde who's going to help you spend your retirement years?" she teased.

He laughed. "Yeah, a gorgeous little blonde. She weighs about three pounds and I call her Miss Kitty."

"You got a cat?"

"It's more like she got me." He threw his pencil on the desk and reared back in his chair. "She showed up at the house yesterday morning. I was sitting on the porch having a cup of coffee and there she was, the scruffiest little tabby cat I've ever seen. Looked like she was half-starving, so I opened a can of tuna and gave it to her."

"You know what they say...feed a cat and you own a cat."

Abe shrugged. "It's all right by me. She's obviously a stray...like me. We can keep each other company in the years I've got left."

"Oh, for heaven's sakes, Abe, you sound like you're dying instead of retiring," she exclaimed.

"I've got to admit that change isn't easy at my age. My whole life has always been the job."

"So what plans do you have?" She was so grateful to have something, anything, to keep her mind off thoughts of Adam.

"I wouldn't mind doing a little work in the private sector...maybe consulting or a little private investigation."

Breanna wished she'd had a private investigator on her payroll the night she'd met Adam. She would have had Adam checked out upside down and inside out before she offered him a word, a glance or a smile.

But it was too late now. She'd already given Adam far more than a smile and she didn't know how to get him out of her thoughts now.

She'd spent the past three days thinking of everything he'd told her. Her heart had ached with the knowledge that now Maggie would never, ever have a connection with the man who had sired her.

And even though Breanna had told herself for a long time that she hated Kurt, she'd been surprised to realize there was a small piece inside her that mourned him, too. That mourning place inside her didn't come from any lingering love, but rather from the compassion of one human being for another.

She was at least grateful for one thing...she was

grateful Adam had stopped their lovemaking in order to tell her the truth about who he was and why he was in town. But it disturbed her that knowing the truth did nothing to staunch the hunger he'd awakened inside her. Knowing the truth did nothing to erase the desire she still felt to be with him intimately.

She was equally conflicted when it came to the knowledge that Kurt's parents were alive and well and had enough money to buy the entire town of Cherokee Corners. She couldn't just forget all the things Kurt had told her about them and the things he'd had to say weren't particularly pleasant.

She wondered if Adam had already told them about Maggie, wondered if at any moment she would be served with legal papers or get a phone call demanding some sort of visitation.

The thought of sharing Maggie with people who would be ashamed of her heritage stirred a rebellion in Breanna that would not be easily overcome.

She told herself Maggie didn't need anyone else in her life, and what the Randolfs didn't know wouldn't hurt them. Let them grieve for their son and let them leave her and Maggie alone. They had nothing that Breanna and Maggie needed, and Breanna certainly had nothing to give to them.

It was after one when she pulled into her driveway and saw Adam seated on his porch. She kept her gaze carefully averted from him as she got out of her car and approached her front door.

She'd just reached her front porch when she heard his footsteps coming toward her. She tensed and reached into her purse.

"Please don't tell me you're getting your gun," he said from just behind her. "I keep telling you if you point that at me often enough one of these times you're going to accidentally shoot me.''

She turned to look at him as she pulled her keys from her purse. ''And what makes you think it would be an accident?'' she asked coolly.

She unlocked her door then turned back to face him. It was difficult to look at him and not remember how masterful his mouth had felt against hers. It was difficult not to remember how his naked chest had felt against her own. It was hard to forget how much of a support he'd been to her in the brief time they'd known each other. ''What do you want, Adam? It's late.''

''We need to talk, Breanna. Can I come in for just a few minutes?''

She wanted to tell him no, she wanted to tell him to just go away and leave her alone, but she knew that sooner or later he would want to talk and decided to just get it over with. ''I really can't imagine what you might have to say to me, but I'll give you fifteen minutes.''

He followed her inside where she dropped her purse on the sofa, then turned to face him, arms crossed defensively over her chest. ''You said we need to talk...so talk.''

He frowned, as if aware that she wasn't open to hearing anything he had to say. He took a step forward, his arms stretched out toward her, but stopped as she took a step backward. His arms fell helplessly to his sides

She didn't want him close enough to her that she would be able to smell his distinctive scent, feel the heat from his body. She didn't want her brain muddied by the desire for him that refused to die despite her wish to the contrary.

"Breanna," he began softly. "Nothing I did from the moment I arrived here was done in an effort to cause you pain in any way."

She eyed him accusingly. "You lied to me by not telling me who you were."

He nodded. "I guess that's true, but the first night I met you, I thought you were a prostitute. I decided to wait to tell you who I was and why I was here until I knew more about you."

"By the next morning you knew I wasn't a prostitute, that I was a cop and came from a good family," she countered.

"I know," he agreed. He dragged a hand across his lower jaw, then raked it through his curly hair. "And I should have told you then, but I didn't. I wanted to make sure you would be open to having a relationship with Uncle Edward and Aunt Anita."

"Have you told them about me...about Maggie?" Fear surged up inside her.

"No. I don't want to tell them until I have your agreement that you'll let them be a part of Maggie's life."

"Then you're going to wait a long time." Exhausted, she sank to the edge of the sofa.

He eyed her in obvious frustration. "Why? Why would you deny a couple the opportunity to bond with their only grandchild? And why would you deny Maggie the opportunity to have more love in her life? Is your hatred for Kurt so great that you would seek revenge on his parents...on your own daughter?"

"I'm not seeking revenge on anyone," she scoffed irritably. "I'm protecting myself...and Maggie."

"From what?" he asked incredulously. He sat down next to her on the sofa, not so close as to be a threat, but as if her words had taken the strength out of his legs. His beautiful blue eyes eyed her searchingly. "What are you afraid of, Bree? For God's sake, tell me what is going through your head."

To her horror, tears stung her eyes. She had tried so hard to forget the horrible things Kurt had said to her when he was leaving. She'd shoved his words deep into the dark recesses of her mind where she believed they would no longer have the power to hurt her. But Adam's questions brought all the pain, all the fear back to the forefront of her mind.

She turned her head away from him, angry that the tears appeared to be out of her control. She felt him move closer to her on the sofa and she wanted to scream at him to get away, to leave her house and allow her the privacy she suddenly needed.

"Bree." His voice was achingly soft and he placed a hand on her arm.

She jerked her arm away, swiped at her falling tears and turned to glare at him. "What difference does it make to you? Why do you care?"

"Because I love my aunt and uncle, because they've lost their only son and I know the knowledge that they have a grandchild will help ease some of their grief, will give them a reason to go on." His eyes grew dark. "My God, Breanna. Where's your compassion?" His voice took on a hard edge that stirred the anger in her.

"Where's *my* compassion?" She jumped up from the sofa and faced him. "Excuse me if my compassion is spent on my daughter rather than two wealthy people who will probably only make her ashamed of her heritage!''

"Ashamed of her heritage?" Adam stood as well, confusion twisting his features. "What in the hell are you talking about?"

"I'm talking about the two people who raised Kurt." Tears raced frantically down her cheeks. "Before Kurt left, he told me that it was a good thing his parents were dead, that it would kill them if they knew their grandchild was going to be a little papoose from a half-breed.

"Don't you understand? Leaving me wasn't the worst thing Kurt did, but making me ashamed of who I am was, and I won't let his parents do the same to my daughter. I won't!" Sobs choked in her throat at the same time Adam reached out and roughly pulled her tight against his chest.

Chapter 10

Adam held her as she cried with a depth of pain that horrified him. He'd always believed his love for his cousin was unconditional.

But as he felt Breanna's pain racking her body with deep sobs, as her words echoed around and around in his head, he realized there was a part of him that didn't like his cousin at all. There was a part of him where a rich anger had been growing for years and now threatened to explode.

This wasn't just a nasty mess Kurt had left behind. This was a real woman, with real emotions and real pain intentionally inflicted by a man Adam had believed he'd loved.

He held her tight, as if the circle of his arms could somehow staunch the pain, stop her tears. He didn't try to speak to her, knew she was beyond listening. He also knew instinctively that the tears she spilled now had probably been balled up inside of her for years.

She cried with her arms around his neck, her face buried in the front of his shirt as she leaned weakly against him. As his shirt grew damp, he wondered how many tears a woman could cry…a thousand…a million?

As the minutes passed, her sobs became less intense and she finally pulled away from him and once again sank down to the sofa. Her eyes were red-rimmed and utterly hollow.

Adam sat next to her and took her hand in his, grateful when she didn't fight him and pull her hand away. "Over the years, my aunt and uncle and I used many adjectives when describing Kurt. He was flighty and unfocused, adventurous and easily bored. We should have been using the truthful adjectives…like irresponsible and lazy and cruel."

The truth seared through him, destroying any illusions he'd ever entertained about Kurt. It was one thing to grieve a man who had died, quite another to grieve for a man who had never existed.

"I've spent my life following behind Kurt, cleaning up whatever chaos he'd left behind…and there was always plenty of chaos."

A deep-seated anger rose to the surface as he thought of the time, the energy that was spent on Kurt's life. "I tried to be a mentor, a role model of sorts, but instead I became his keeper. But you can't blame my aunt Anita and uncle Edward for the kind of man Kurt was. They are good, decent people who would be appalled by Kurt's words to you."

She sighed and pulled her hand from his. "Kurt told me his parents were dead, but he also told me they had been selfish, mean people who only believed in the almighty dollar. He told me that, before their deaths, they had tried to control him and if they'd been alive when Maggie was born, they would have used their power and influence to take her away from me, to make her into the image of themselves."

"I neglected to mention another adjective that obviously described Kurt." Pain shot through Adam. "He was a liar who used lies to manipulate people into doing what he wanted."

Breanna leaned her head back and closed her eyes. "I don't know what to believe. I've read articles about Edward and Anita Randolf. I know they're wealthy and high-society. How can I trust that they aren't the people Kurt thought they were." She opened her eyes and gazed at Adam once again.

"I'm not going to lie to you. They are wealthy...incredibly wealthy, but that doesn't make them bad people. I was a grieving eleven-year-old when they opened up their house, their hearts to me. They loved me like a son and made me a part of their family."

He could see she still didn't believe him. "Breanna, Kurt lied about them being dead, he apparently lied when he said his marriage vows to you, how can you believe anything he told you?"

She sighed again. "I don't know, Adam. I don't know what to believe about anything anymore."

Once again he reached out and took her hand in his. "I'll make you a deal. I won't tell my aunt and uncle about Maggie until you give me the okay. But, in the meantime, I want you to consider it. They need her, Breanna, and I promise you won't be sorry if you give them a chance to be a part of her life."

"I just…I need some time," she finally said.

He nodded, then tightened his grip on her hand. "I've missed talking to you the past couple of days."

"I've been very angry with you."

"As you should have been," he agreed. "I just need you to understand that I didn't mean to betray your trust. I didn't mean to hurt you."

She said nothing, but the hollow look in her eyes seemed to fill with a touch of warmth. "The phone calls have stopped," she said, changing the subject.

"They have?" He eyed her in surprise.

"I didn't receive another one after I hooked up the caller ID."

"That's odd, isn't it? Who did you tell about the ID?" She seemed to have forgotten that her hand was still in his. He liked the feel of her hand, so small and dainty and swallowed by his bigger one.

"My family…my partner. Why?"

"I just think it's weird that the calls stopped the minute you got the ID box."

"I figured either it was Michael Rivers and our little discussion with him backed him off, or it was somebody pranking and they got bored. I don't care exactly what happened, I'm just grateful the calls have stopped." She pulled her hand away from his and stood. "It's late, Adam, and I think we've said everything that needs to be said."

He stood and followed her to the front door. She looked small and vulnerable and when he thought of the things Kurt had said to her, his blood boiled hot in his veins.

When they got to her front door, he paused just inside, wanting…needing to touch her in some way, erase the memory of Kurt's hurtful words.

She looked up at him, her eyes dark and achingly beautiful. "You said before that you've spent your life cleaning up Kurt's messes. Is that what I am to you? A mess that needs to be taken care of, a problem that had to be resolved?"

A swift denial leaped to his lips, but didn't make it out of his mouth. "I came to Cherokee Corners with that in mind, that you were the final loose end...the final mess that Kurt had left behind." He saw that his words cut her and he quickly continued, "But it took me exactly one day to realize you were far, far more than a mess for me to clean up."

Cautiously, he reached out a hand and touched a strand of her shining hair. "The warmth of your family touched me and Maggie has utterly charmed me. And you...from the moment I saw you, you took my breath away. If I could, I'd take away all the things Kurt said to you that caused you pain. If I could, I'd make it so nobody would ever hurt you again."

She was in his arms then, her lips raised to his and he kissed her with a fervor he hadn't known existed inside him. Her mouth was hot and eager against his, but she broke the kiss abruptly and stepped back from him.

She shut the front door and locked them inside, then looked up at him, her eyes filled with a want that made him weak inside.

"I don't know if I really even like you anymore, Adam Spencer," she said softly. "And I certainly don't completely trust you. But I want you, and I haven't wanted a man since Kurt left me years ago. Still, I need you to understand that if we sleep together, it will just be sex...it doesn't change my mind about anything where you are concerned."

For a moment Adam was speechless. "That's fine with me," he finally said. "I told you from the very beginning the last thing I want is any sort of a long-term relationship. But I do want you."

He barely got the words out of his mouth before they were in each other's arms, kissing with a depth of emotion that made second thought impossible, threw caution to the wind.

As his lips possessed hers, he knew nothing and nobody was going to stop them tonight. The world could crash down around their heads, but he was going to make love to Breanna James.

Breanna would like to believe that she'd been gripped by some sort of temporary insanity, but the truth was she hadn't made love with a man since Kurt had left her nearly six years before. Her body ached with the need to be held, to be caressed, to be loved, and in the six years since Kurt's desertion no man had tempted her in the least…until Adam.

As their lips clung together, he started moving them out of the foyer and toward the stairs, but she stopped him. She didn't want him in her bed, didn't want the implied intimacy of him in her personal space.

Instead she kicked off her shoes and led him into the living room, where she turned out all the lights, leaving the room illuminated by a shaft of moonlight that danced through gauzy curtains.

Their kiss broke and she sank to the floor, motioning him to join her on the soft, lush carpeting. She didn't have to motion twice. He sank down to his knees facing her and cupped her face with his hands. In his eyes she saw a feverish need that would have wiped away any lingering doubts she might have entertained.

It was obvious he wanted her, but she was doing this for herself. It was a selfish act, feeding her own need to be held, to pretend for just a little while that she was loved.

His hands moved from her face down her shoulders, then cupped her breasts. She could feel the heat of his hands through her wispy bra and thin T-shirt. Her nipples tingled and hardened in response to the intimate touch.

She ran her hands across the broad width of his shoulders, over the muscles of his chest and down the flat of his stomach. He sucked in his breath, as if finding her touch a delicious torment.

In one smooth movement, he reached down, grabbed the bottom of her T-shirt and pulled it off over her head. Her heart raced and she felt as if she were burning up with fever as his lips claimed hers in a deep, hot kiss.

She tugged at his shirt, wanting to feel his naked skin beneath her fingertips. He quickly unbuttoned the shirt and shrugged it off his shoulders, then reached around her to unsnap her bra.

As the wisp of lace fell away, he pulled her tight against him and she reveled in the feel of her naked skin against his. His skin was hot and she felt herself melting into him, as if they were fusing together.

Gently, he laid her back on the carpeting then his fingers worked the snap fastener on her slacks. As he pulled down her slacks, she aided him by raising her hips. He stood, leaving her there clad only in her pink silk bikini panties.

She watched as he kicked off his shoes, pulled off

his socks, then tore off his pants, leaving him only in a pair of briefs that did nothing to disguise the extent of his desire for her.

He rejoined her on the floor, gathering her in his arms as his mouth hungrily devoured hers. His hips moved against hers, the friction of his hardness even through the barrier of their underclothing driving her half-wild with desire.

He raised his head to look at her, his eyes filled with a wildness that thrummed through her. ''You are so beautiful,'' he said, his voice deep and husky.

''So are you,'' she replied. Her hands splayed across the width of his back, loving the way his muscles bunched and played beneath her fingertips. ''I love the way your skin feels against mine.''

He slid his mouth down the length of her throat and captured one of her nipples. As he rolled his tongue over the tip, pinpricks of fire exploded in her veins, radiating out from her breast deep into the very center of her being. He looked at her once again. ''I love the way you taste,'' he said, then tasted her some more, moving his mouth to her other breast.

By the time he was finished nipping and licking her skin down to the waistband of her panties, she was delirious with want. But he seemed to be in no hurry to complete the act.

''Breanna,'' he said, his voice seeming to come from far away. ''I…I don't have anything with me.''

She frowned, trying to surface from the dizzying haze to understand what he was talking about. When realization set in, rather than upset her, it relieved her. He hadn't come here with a condom in his pocket, which indicated seduction hadn't been on his mind.

''It's all right,'' she replied. ''I'm on the pill.'' She

mentally thanked the doctor who had placed her on the pill three years ago due to irregular periods.

She barely got the words out of her mouth when he touched her through the thin material of her panties and she cried out in exquisite pleasure.

Then her panties were gone and he touched her bareness with quick light strokes that swept her higher and higher, moved her to a release that left her shuddering and clinging to him with panting gasps. Her body felt like liquid, boneless and spent, but more than anything she wanted to return the pleasure.

She plucked at his briefs and he pulled them down and kicked them off, leaving him as naked as her. She gripped him, reveling in his throbbing hardness and as she stroked her hand up the length of him, he moaned deep in the back of his throat.

His mouth sought hers again, hot and hungry as she continued to move her hand over him. He groaned and shoved her hand away, then rolled over on top of her, poised to possess her completely.

Before he entered her, his eyes held hers and she felt as if he were making love to her there first...with those beautiful blue eyes of his. Then he slipped into her and she closed her eyes, unable to hold them open as wave after wave of pleasure suffused her.

Slowly at first, he moved deep within her, then pulled back, each stroke a pleasure that threatened to shatter her into a thousand pieces.

She clung to him like a drowning woman, meeting his thrusts with a need of her own. It had never been this way for her before. She'd never felt so lost...and so found, so needy and yet so fulfilled. The depth of emotion, both mental and physical that filled her both frightened and excited her.

Faster and faster he moved against her, into her, stoking the flames of her passion higher…higher. A new tension built inside her as her muscles tensed in expectation…anticipation.

He cried out her name and she loved the sound of his voice, graveled and thick with emotion. Just as she reached the peak of a second release, he stiffened against her and shuddered with his own.

For a long moment they remained in each other's arms, the only sound in the room their breaths working to slow to a more normal pace.

He finally leaned up and gazed down at her, his eyes warm as the sky on a sunny day. Gently he swept a strand of her hair from her cheek, then leaned down and kissed her lips lingeringly.

The sweet gentleness of his kiss touched her as much as anything else they had shared and she tried to throw up mental defenses against him.

When the kiss ended he smiled at her. "I feel like a teenager."

"What do you mean?" Her heart was finally finding a normal rhythm although she loved the feel of his skin against hers.

"I feel like your parents are upstairs in bed and we're sneaking a bout of lovemaking on their living-room floor. I've even got the rug burns on my knees to prove it."

She laughed. "This would never have happened in my parents' house. All the boys in town knew my father was chief of police and wouldn't hesitate to shoot them if they tried something like this." She rolled away from him and sat up. "I'm going to go take a shower."

"I'm a great back scrubber," he said.

Breanna had intended her statement to indicate to him that it was time for him to go. But, it was obvious he wasn't ready to call it a night and looking at the heat in his eyes, she realized neither was she.

"A woman can always use a good back scrubber," she replied, surprised to discover she was half-breathless again.

Within minutes they were standing beneath a hot, steamy spray of water in the bathroom off Breanna's bedroom. She had never showered with a man before, had no idea what to expect. But he led the way, soaping up a sponge and running it across her back.

At first it seemed he intended to do just what he'd said...scrub her back. But it didn't take long before he was raking that sponge not just across her back, but across her breasts, over her thighs and down her legs. And then the sponge was gone and it was his soapy hands exciting her back to a fever pitch.

They made love again with Breanna pressed against the glass enclosure, the warmth of the water and steam and the slickness of their soapy bodies enhancing the pleasure.

Afterward, Breanna pulled on a robe as Adam redressed. Regret swept through her as she silently watched him. She'd thought she could make love to him and enjoy the physical release it would bring without being touched emotionally.

But she realized now this man had managed to crawl beneath her defenses. Despite the fact that he'd kept his real identity a secret from her, in spite of the fact that he'd come here simply to tie up any loose ends Kurt had left behind, he'd managed to get inside her heart in a way that frightened her.

He made her almost willing to believe in the

dreams she'd once entertained…the dreams of love forever, of a strong and happy marriage…of a family all her own. Fool's illusion, she reminded herself. Illusions bred in the afterglow of beautiful lovemaking.

What she needed most now was distance from him and from the foolishness of her own thoughts. She was grateful he didn't mention spending the night. She didn't want to spend her sleeping hours in his arms, didn't want to awaken in his warm embrace.

"You know this changes nothing," she said as she followed him downstairs to her front door.

"What do you mean?" He reached the door and turned to look at her.

"I mean I still don't want you to tell your aunt and uncle about Maggie." She pulled her robe closer around her, threatened by how much she wanted to grab him by the hand and lead him back up to her bedroom. To sleep, to dream in his arms would be heaven, but it would only make things more difficult in the end…and there was an end.

"Breanna, I told you I wouldn't tell them until you're ready for me to, but you're wrong when you say that nothing has changed."

"What do you mean?" She eyed him curiously, wondering how it was possible he could look so devastatingly handsome with his hair in curly disarray and a five o'clock shadow decorating his jaw.

He opened the front door, then leaned over and kissed her on the cheek. As he straightened up, in her eyes he saw the flames of a fire not yet sated. "As far as I'm concerned everything has changed. Now I don't have to imagine what your body feels like against mine, I know. And I don't have to try to imagine the sound of your sweet sighs while I make love to you, because I know. And most important of all what's changed is that I now know how much I love making love to you and I know I want to do it again...and again.''

His words made her heart flutter with a combination of sweet anticipation and anxiety. ''Adam, tonight was wonderful...beautiful, but wouldn't it be foolish for us to repeat the experience?''

''Why would it be foolish?'' His eyes held her gaze intently.

Because I'm falling in love with you, she wanted to say. Because ultimately it would be like Kurt all over again...only this time it would be worse because Adam was on the verge of capturing her heart in a way Kurt never had. But the end result would be that he'd walk away, just as Kurt had done.

She grabbed the ends of her belt and pulled it tighter. ''Adam, it's late and at the moment I'm too tired to think.''

Once again he leaned down, this time to kiss her gently on the temple. ''Goodnight, Bree,'' he said softly. ''May sweet, happy dreams be yours.'' With these words he turned and left her house.

She closed the door after him and knew she didn't have to worry about the danger of any strange phone calls. The danger to her was much closer...right next door in the form of one handsome Adam Spencer.

Chapter 11

Sunday was one of those picture-perfect spring days. The morning sky was cloudless, but there was just enough of a breeze to keep the sun from feeling overly warm.

Adam dressed in a pair of jeans and a light blue polo shirt, then climbed into his car and headed out for the Cultural Center. He wasn't sure what time the festivities would start there, but he didn't want to miss anything.

More than anything, he didn't want to miss seeing Breanna. He hadn't seen her at all the day before. Her car had been gone when he'd gotten up yesterday morning and she hadn't come home after work.

With Alyssa's premonition of danger still in his head, he'd gotten worried when she hadn't come home after work. On a hunch he'd driven by her parents' home, relieved to see her car parked there. He went back to the cottage, knowing she was safe.

She was safe, but obviously avoiding him. He frowned as he rolled down the window to allow in some of the fresh, sweet scented spring air. Maybe she regretted their lovemaking. While he thought making love had not been the wisest decision they could have made, there was no way he could regret what had been so fantastic, so magical.

Making love to her had filled an emptiness he hadn't realized he possessed. She'd been an eager participant, a generous lover. But he knew all about dawn regrets and suspected that's what had kept her from her home the day before.

Hopefully when he saw her today there would be no awkwardness between them and he wouldn't see the darkness of regret in her lovely eyes.

The parking lot of the Cultural Center was already nearly full when he arrived. He spied Breanna's car parked in one of the spaces nearest the building and was surprised to feel his pulse quicken.

The Cultural Center building was void of people, but large doors opened to allow entry to the back of the property where Adam realized the festivities were taking place.

A large crowd of visitors were gathered around a huge open area. At the far end of the area was a deep pit and he could see the flames of fire coming from within the pit. There were seven arbors encircling the fire and he wondered the significance of them.

He joined the crowd of spectators just as the drums began beating rhythmically. His gaze shot around, trying to catch a glimpse of Breanna and Maggie. He saw them standing on the other side of the large expanse of dirt and he took a moment to drink in Breanna's stunning appearance.

She wore a dress in a calico print material. Bright blue material formed a series of diamond shapes around the yoke and on the skirt. The dress had three-quarter-length sleeves and ended at her calves. Her feet were bare and her hair was braided in two thick shiny braids, the ends of which rested on her breasts.

She looked proud and strong and achingly beautiful and he wondered how in the hell Kurt had been able to turn his back on her and walk away. Adam knew with a certainty it had been a flaw in Kurt, not Breanna, that had ruined their marriage.

Maggie stood next to her mother, clad in an outfit identical to Breanna's, except on Maggie's little legs were the shells that Adam knew would be part of one of the ceremonial dances.

It was Maggie who saw him first and her smile was as bright as the sky. She waved, then tugged at her mother's dress and pointed to him.

Breanna raised a hand in a greeting, then returned her attention to the dancers who had begun to perform. Adam tried to watch the dancers, but found his attention wandering again and again to Breanna.

He felt the rhythmic bang of the drums thrumming deep in his veins. It was a primitive beat of timelessness, of a proud people with a rich culture and traditions.

He could tell that Breanna felt the drums inside her as well. Her slender body swayed slightly with each beat and one of her feet tapped on the ground. He wanted to go to her, to move with her to the beat that sang in her soul, to learn the mysteries of her heritage.

When the dance ended and the drums had stilled, Rita stood in the center of the circle. Like her daughter she was clad in a traditional dress and the crowd stilled as she raised her hands for silence.

For the next few minutes she educated the group, explaining to them that the seven arbors surrounding the ceremonial fire represented the seven clans, Wolf, Wild Potato, War Paint, Bird Clan, Long Hair, Deer and Blue. She then entertained with several legends Adam found fascinating. When she was finished, more dancing resumed.

Adam made his way around the ceremonial circle to where Breanna and Maggie were standing. "Adam, did you come to watch me dance?" Maggie asked eagerly when he'd reached them.

"I wouldn't have missed it," he replied, obviously to the little girl's delight. He then smiled at Breanna. "Hi."

"Hi, yourself," she replied. Before they could say anything else to each other Rita arrived to greet Adam.

"Adam, it's nice to see you here," she said. "Are you enjoying everything?"

"Definitely. I'm finding it both entertaining and educational."

Rita smiled in obvious satisfaction. "That's exactly what we're hoping for with these festivals. We want people to enjoy them, but we'd like to teach a little of the Cherokee ways at the same time."

"You're doing a remarkable job," Adam replied, noticing that Breanna had moved with Maggie closer to the circle apparently in preparation of Maggie's performance.

"And what are you doing, Adam Spencer?" Her dark eyes held his gaze and in those eyes he saw the love of a mother worried for her daughter.

He didn't pretend not to know what she was asking. He was fairly certain Breanna would have told her mother everything…at least up to the point of their lovemaking.

"I'm not sure," he admitted softly, his gaze once again seeking Breanna. "It seemed clear-cut and simple in the beginning. Find Breanna, make sure she and Maggie were doing all right, then go back to Kansas City and let Kurt's parents know they have a grandchild."

"And now it isn't so simple?"

He looked back at Rita and sighed. "No, it isn't. She doesn't want me to tell Kurt's parents about Maggie."

Rita's eyes were suddenly filled with sad wisdom. "Your cousin took much more from my daughter than her heart. He took her pride as a Cherokee, her pride as a woman and left her with an anger that still burns far too bright."

"But she's angry at the wrong people," Adam said. "She's denying two loving people the chance to love her daughter."

"Give her time," Rita said. "She's had almost six years believing Kurt had no family, that his parents when alive had been bad people. She's only had a week to process the fact that he lied about something so basic."

Adam nodded, but there was a part of him that was afraid to give her too much more time. He felt himself being drawn closer and closer into her life, into her family and into a world he'd never wanted for himself.

At that moment the Cherokee Stomp Dance began and Adam watched as Maggie participated in the ceremonial dance of her people. Several times during her performance she smiled at Adam, as if she were performing specifically for him alone. Breanna had disappeared and Adam returned his attention to little Maggie.

When she was finished, she came running to his side. "Did you see me, Adam?" She took hold of his hand. "Did you see me be a shell-shaker?"

"I did." He returned her smile, finding it impossible not to. Her eyes sparkled with excitement and her round cheeks were flushed with color.

"Did you like it?" she asked.

"I thought you were the best shell-shaker I've ever seen."

She tugged his hand, forcing him to lean down closer to her. "If you wanted to, you could tell me that you're proud of me." He looked at her in surprise, finding her words odd. "When my friend, Jenny, dances for her daddy, he always tells her he's proud of her."

Adam's heart constricted in his chest as he gazed at Maggie's pretty little face and the hungry look in her eyes. "I am very proud of you, little one," he said softly. "But you know I'm not your daddy."

She leaned against him and nodded. "I know. My mommy told me my daddy died. I feel sad about it, but I think the best thing to do would be to get another daddy."

She gazed up at him with serious gray eyes. "My daddy wasn't really that good anyway...I mean I never saw him or talked to him. The next one I get I want him to live with me and talk to me and maybe sometimes even give me a hug and tell me he's proud."

Adam's heart swelled up in his chest, momentarily making speech impossible. What simple things would make a little girl happy, make her feel as if her life was complete. It was positively criminal, what Kurt had left behind.

"Until you find that new daddy, how about I give you a hug and tell you I'm proud of you." Adam leaned down and Maggie wrapped her arms around his neck. He squeezed her tightly, then released her and straightened up.

Eventually, Breanna would find a man to be a part of her life, to become a loving, caring stepfather for Maggie. But that man wasn't him. Still, he knew somehow he would never be the same when he left Cherokee Corners and this family behind.

Breanna had been helping the other women set food on the long tables near the back of the building. She looked up just in time to see Adam give Maggie a hug. The sight of the big, handsome man hugging her daughter brought forth a pang of pain in her heart.

When Kurt had left her, she had closed her heart to the possibility of ever again having a man in her life. But in doing that, was she being unfair to her daughter, who seemed to be so hungry for a father figure? Was she ultimately punishing Maggie by guarding her own heart?

She shoved away these disturbing thoughts and went back to work, setting out platters and dishes of both traditional and contemporary fare to feed the spectators. Coleslaw sat beside the traditional grape dumplings, a loaf of French bread was next to a platter of fry bread. There was fried chicken, roast beef, macaroni salads and beans. The women had been busy for the past week preparing dishes for this event.

Within minutes the food was ready and the spectators moved around the tables filling their plates. ''Are you going to avoid me all day?''

She whirled around to see Adam standing just behind her and was irritated at the way her heart leapt in her chest. ''I'm not avoiding you, I've just been busy,'' she countered.

He smiled knowingly and to her surprise she felt a blush warm her cheeks. ''Okay,'' she admitted, ''perhaps I've been avoiding you a little.''

''Why?''

She couldn't tell him the truth, that she was falling in love with him and needed to distance herself from him. ''I don't know,'' she hedged. ''I guess a bit of morning-after embarrassment.''

''There's nothing to be embarrassed about,'' he returned. ''We're two consenting adults who shared something special. And what I'd like to do now is share the day with you and Maggie.''

She wanted to say yes...she wanted to say no. She wanted him to stay, she wanted him to leave. Before she could reply, Maggie raced up between them and grabbed his hand and hers. ''Are you both going to watch me play *A-ne-jo-di* after lunch?''

Adam looked at Breanna questioningly. ''It's a form of stickball. The young people play several games this afternoon.''

He looked down at Maggie. ''I'd be delighted to watch you play your game, especially if your mother will watch with me.''

''You will, right, Mommy? You and Adam together and you can cheer for me.''

Breanna shot a quick glare to Adam, knowing he'd intentionally manipulated her. "Yes, Maggie, we'll watch you together…now go get something to eat so you have plenty of energy to play." As Maggie ran off to fix a plate, Breanna looked at Adam once again. "That wasn't very nice."

"What?" His clear blue eyes held a teasing pretense of innocence.

"You know what," she replied. "You manipulated me by using my daughter."

"You're right," he agreed with an irritating, dashing smile. His smile faded and he gazed at her with naked honesty. "Breanna, can't we just spend some time together today? I enjoy your company and it won't be long before I'll be returning home to Kansas City."

His words shot through her. Of course he would be leaving Cherokee Corners and returning home. He'd never indicated anything to the contrary. He'd made it more than clear on several occasions that he had no intention of getting married, of having any children.

But why not just enjoy the day, a little voice said inside her head. Why not just take this day to enjoy his company? "Fine," she finally said. "The first thing I intend to do is eat. You're welcome to join me."

Ten minutes later they sat at one of the picnic tables to eat. All around them people chatted to one another and the whoops and hollers of kids at play filled the air.

"I saw my mother talking to you earlier," Breanna said. "Did she give you one of her standard educational lessons?"

He grinned, looking achingly handsome with the sunshine playing on his hair and emphasizing the sculptured planes of his face. "No, no lessons, we just visited for a few minutes. Your father had a little talk with me, too."

Breanna looked at him in surprise. "About what?"

He smiled wryly. "The gist of our conversation was that if I hurt you in any way, the wrath of the entire James family would come down upon my head."

Breanna groaned. "I can't believe he did that."

Adam shrugged. "He's your father. He wants the best for you and doesn't want to see anything make you sad or unhappy."

"I'm twenty-seven years old...old enough to take care of myself," she replied. "Besides, you don't have the power to hurt me. You've made it clear you aren't in the market for a relationship and I've made it clear that I'm not, either."

"Good," he replied. "Then I don't have to worry about anyone from your family meeting me in a dark alley with a gun?"

She smiled. "It depends on what you're doing in that dark alley."

"You told me your sister usually takes part in these festivities, but I haven't seen her here today," he said.

"Apparently there was a break in the murder case she's been working on so she couldn't come." For the next few minutes they ate in silence, although she noticed Adam taking in the ambiance of the gathering.

"There's such a strong sense of community here," he said later as they walked toward the field where the *A-ne-jo-di* games would be played. "You mentioned the other night that the worst thing Kurt had done to you was make you ashamed of your heritage. What did you mean?''

Breanna sighed and stared out to the field where the players were gathering. In her mind's eye she saw Kurt on their wedding day. They'd married at city hall, a spur-of-the-moment action that Breanna would later regret.

On that day Kurt's gray eyes had glittered with a sense of adventure that had been infectious, and in his eyes she thought she had seen the promise of a lifetime of love and commitment.

Aware that Adam was waiting for her to say something, she searched through her mind to find the right words to explain the depth of the trauma his cousin had left behind.

''At first, Kurt seemed to take a genuine interest in the Cherokee culture. He encouraged me to tell him about our belief system, our legends and our way of life both now and in the past.''

She looked at Adam, surprised to discover that the pain that had once lingered in her heart whenever she thought of Kurt, was far less intense, rather like the echo of a song she'd heard long ago. ''I was thrilled to share with him, felt as if his interest was because he loved me. I didn't realize that to him it was simply a weapon to later use against me.''

''What do you mean?'' His question was nearly drowned out by the crowd's cheers as the game on the field began.

She waited for the cheers to die down and continued to stare out at the field. ''It wasn't long before he was making fun of our legends, scorning our belief system and mocking our ceremonies. He began to call me his little savage, his squaw woman.'' The memory of her humiliation warmed her cheeks.

"I have never been so ashamed in my life." Adam's voice was sharp and she looked at him in surprise. "It sickens me to think that I had any kind of a connection to a man who would be capable of doing something like that."

He grabbed her hand. She could tell by the expression on his face, the desperate empathy as he squeezed her hand, that he meant what he said. He looked ill with disgust, revolted by what she'd just shared with him.

"By the time he finally left, I felt as if there was something wrong with me...like I was a dirty savage."

Adam's gaze turned to one of surprise. "But you're such a strong woman, such a smart woman. How could he make you believe those kinds of things about yourself?"

She pulled her hand from his and waved to Maggie. "I don't know." She looked at him once again. "Lots of smart, proud, strong women become the victims of mental abuse. I was pregnant, probably hormonal and desperate to maintain a relationship with the father of my baby. Besides, Kurt's mental abuse began subtly and built over the months."

Once again she directed her gaze to the field. "If he hadn't left when he did, eventually I would have left him."

"I'm sorry, Bree. Dear God, I'm so sorry." His deep voice was laced with pain.

She smiled at him ruefully. "You cleaned up his messes, you tried to keep him out of trouble, you even feel bad about the things he did. Tell me, Adam, what did you get out of it?''

He frowned at her in bewilderment. "What do you mean?"

"I mean, in any kind of a relationship there is give and take. It's obvious Kurt did a lot of taking, so what did you get from your relationship with him?"

He laughed and in the laughter he sounded distinctly uncomfortable. "This is far too serious a conversation to be having on such a beautiful day in the middle of a festival."

"You're right," she agreed. She wasn't even sure why she'd told the ugly details of her marriage to Kurt, and she certainly couldn't figure out why she felt the need to understand his relationship to Kurt.

Too close. She was already far too close to him for comfort and she wasn't thinking about his physical proximity at the moment.

He had gotten far too deep into her heart, far too much under her skin. It was far too easy when she was with him to remember the dreams she'd once entertained, the dreams of a happy, passionate marriage and a loving family of her own.

Already she knew that when he left he would leave her heart in pain. Each day, every moment, every second he remained only cut her heart more deeply. It was time to put an end to whatever it was the two of them had been sharing. It was time to say goodbye.

Chapter 12

It was almost ten when Adam got into his car to follow Breanna and Maggie home from the Cultural Center. As he kept their taillights in his sight, the enjoyment of the day filled his soul.

After the stickball games there had been more dancing, more singing and celebration. More legends had been told, more education given on the Cherokee people and their past. There had been much laughter and talk as old friendships were renewed and new friendships were made.

Watching Breanna interact, talking with animation, laughing in abandon and joyously singing had been a delight.

By evening it seemed that all the town of Cherokee Corners had come to the Cultural Center to join in the fun. Adam saw many of the people who had been at the James's barbecue.

Jacob Kincaid, the owner of the bank had sat for a

little while with them and they had talked about the growth of the city. They'd been joined by Glen Cleberg, the chief of police, who had bemoaned the fact that the city was outgrowing the police department.

Savannah arrived late in the evening, disappointed that the lead they'd received in their murder case had gone nowhere. The police were back to square one, with the naked body of the murdered Greg Maxwell found in front of the city library and no clues as to the perpetrator of the crime.

He and Breanna had not had any time for personal conversation the rest of the day, but her question to him about Kurt had played and replayed in his mind.

What had he gotten from his relationship from Kurt? What had kept him cleaning up after him, trying to take care of him, and keeping him out of trouble for so many years?

It hadn't been his love and respect for his aunt and uncle that had kept him bailing out Kurt. More than once they had told him to get on with his life, to stop being his cousin's keeper.

Certainly Kurt had never seemed particularly grateful for Adam's support and help. Nor had he ever seemed the least bit contrite for his bad behavior.

So what had Adam gotten out of his relationship with his cousin? He felt as if discovering the answer was important, but it remained just out of his reach no matter how hard he tried to figure it out.

He pulled into the driveway of his cottage as Breanna parked in front of her house. He exited his car, then walked over to where she was getting ready to lift a sleeping Maggie from the back seat.

"Here, let me." He gave her no opportunity to reject his offer but instead gently moved her aside and leaned into the back seat and picked up Maggie in his arms.

The little girl instantly molded herself to him, her arms around his neck and her baby breaths warming his neck.

"Thanks," Breanna murmured, then hurried ahead of him to unlock the front door. "I can take her from here," she said as they walked into the foyer.

"Don't be silly," he countered. "I can take her upstairs for you." Maggie murmured something unintelligible against his neck and he patted her back to reassure her as he walked up the stairs to the second story.

Breanna followed close behind and when he turned into Maggie's room, she quickly pulled down the spread on the bed and motioned for him to place Maggie there.

As he laid Maggie down, her eyes opened and she gave him a sleepy smile. "Hi, Adam," she said.

"Hi, Maggie. You can go back to sleep now. You're home safe and sound."

"Are you going to kiss me good-night?"

Adam leaned down and kissed her softly on her cheek, but before he could stand up again, Maggie placed her hand on his cheek. Her gray eyes were filled with the smiles of youth. "If you ever need a little girl to be a pretend daughter, you could borrow me." Her eyes drifted closed again.

Her words wrapped around Adam's heart and squeezed tight. "Thank you, sweetie, I'll keep that in mind," he whispered softly. He straightened up and turned to leave, his gaze meeting Breanna's. He found her expression positively inscrutable.

He watched as she kissed her daughter good-night,

covered her with the sheet, then he followed her back down the stairs.

"Where's Rachel?" he asked when they were in the living room. "Is she still staying with your sister?"

"She was until yesterday. She left early yesterday morning to go to Tulsa. Her father is in a nursing home there. She'll be back sometime tomorrow." She hesitated a beat. "Want some coffee?"

The question caught him by surprise, but he instantly nodded his agreement. "Sounds good." Of course, what he wanted was far more than coffee.

He wanted a repeat of what they'd shared two nights before. He wanted to unbraid her hair and work his fingers through the strands. He wanted to slide her dress from her body and make love to every inch of her silken skin.

He had enjoyed casual, intimate affairs in the past, but he couldn't remember ever wanting a woman with the intensity that he wanted Breanna.

However, during the last hours of the festival, he'd thought he'd felt her withdrawing from him. She'd grown quiet…distant and he'd wished he'd had the capacity to read her mind. He wished it again as he sat at the kitchen table and watched her preparing the coffee to brew.

"I had a great time today," he said. "It seemed like everyone in town was there."

"We usually get good turnouts for the festivals." She reached in the cabinet and withdrew two mugs. "We have three each year, one in the spring, the summer and the fall." She set an empty mug in front of him as the scent of coffee filled the air.

"You okay? You seem sort of quiet."

"I'm fine," she replied. She leaned with her back against the counter and stared at some point just over his head. "I've just been thinking."

"Thinking about what?"

She didn't reply immediately, but instead turned around to grab the coffeepot. She filled his cup, then one for herself, then returned the pot back where it belonged.

"Tell me about being raised by your aunt and uncle." She sat across from him at the table. "Tell me about those years."

He leaned back in the chair and frowned thoughtfully. "I think I already told you that initially when I arrived at Uncle Edward and Aunt Anita's house I was miserable. I was mourning my parents, missing my home, my room…my life. It was summer and I spent a lot of those first days sitting at my bedroom window, certain that I'd never, ever be happy again."

"Did you and your parents live in Kansas City?" she asked.

He shook his head. "St. Louis. It was a five-hour drive from our home in St. Louis to my uncle Edward and aunt Anita's in Kansas City, but for an eleven-year-old kid, it felt as if I'd been transplanted from one country to another."

She wrapped her slender fingers around her coffee mug. "My roots are so firmly entrenched here, I can't imagine what it would be like to have been moved to a new city…a new family at such a young age."

"I was lucky in that there was no way my aunt and uncle were going to allow me to spend my life staring out a window and feeling sorry for myself." He felt the smile that curved his lips as he thought about the lengths his aunt and uncle went to in order to involve him once again in life.

"What did they do?" she asked curiously.

"The first thing they did was sign up Kurt and me for a baseball team. I don't think Uncle Edward had ever even watched a game before in his life, but suddenly he was helping coach and Aunt Anita was providing refreshments and it became a family thing. Kurt hated it, but that summer of baseball games is what made the transition of old life to new easier for me."

"You and Kurt were immediately close?"

Adam frowned thoughtfully. "Even then Kurt was filled with a crazy energy that was both invigorating and exhausting. I was fascinated by him and embraced him as I would have a younger, rather spoiled brother of my own." He cocked his head and looked at her quizzically. "Why all the questions?"

"I've been thinking about Maggie," she finally said. She took a sip of her coffee, her eyes dark. "I've just been thinking about the fact that a child can never have too much love in their life."

Adam said nothing, but he saw the conflicting emotions that swept across her lovely face. She stared into the dark brew of her cup and continued, "There's an old saying about an acorn never falling far from the tree and when I think of that, I'm afraid to allow Kurt's parents into our lives."

She raised a hand to still Adam's protest. "Wait...I'm not finished," she exclaimed. She paused a moment and took a sip of her coffee. "Then, I have to remind myself that Anita and Edward Randolf also raised you and you're nothing like Kurt."

"Well, thank you for that," he said dryly.

She drew a deep breath. "You can tell them, Adam. You can go back to Kansas City and tell them about Maggie."

He heard the whisper of fear in her voice, knew she was conflicted about her decision. He reached across the table and covered her hand with his. "Are you sure that's what you want?"

"No. I'm not sure of anything, except that I have to trust you...to trust your judgment where Kurt's parents are concerned. If what you've said about them is true, then it would be selfish of me to keep them from Maggie...to keep Maggie from them."

"I promise you won't be sorry." Happiness filled Adam as he thought of his aunt and uncle and the joy they'd feel in Maggie's existence. His happiness was quickly followed by the realization that now there was really nothing keeping him here other than Alyssa's vague feeling of danger.

Breanna pulled her hand from his. "So I guess this means you'll be returning to Kansas City very soon."

"Yeah, it will take me a day or so to pack up my things." A hollowness resounded in his chest. He shoved it away and stood, suddenly needing to get out of her kitchen, away from her. "Thanks for the coffee," he said. "I think I'm ready to call it a night. It's been a long day."

She stood as well, obviously surprised by his hasty retreat. She followed him to the front door. "You'll come around and say goodbye to Maggie before you leave?"

"Of course." Goodbye...he'd never dreamed it would be so hard to say to anyone. What was it Alyssa had said...that sometimes loose ends could snarl you all up?

"Good night," he said and quickly walked through the front door, afraid that if he lingered a moment, a mere second, he would want to take her in his arms and kiss her sweet lips. And that would only make goodbye that much more difficult.

And he did intend to say goodbye. He had a life to get back to, a life without the complications of any relationships with any women or children.

He walked into the cottage and sank down on the sofa. Leaning his head back he closed his eyes and remembered little Maggie's bright smile, the offer that if he ever needed a temporary daughter he could borrow her.

It would be easy to love a child like Maggie, whose eyes shone with the promise of the future, who offered love so easily. Had Kurt's parents felt the same way about him when he'd been young?

Had they looked into his bright baby eyes and imagined all the great things he might become, all the wonderful things he might do? Had they lain awake nights dreaming of Kurt's life, with no idea how many tears, how much heartache he would eventually bring to them?

There was no way Adam intended to live what his aunt and uncle had lived, no way in hell he would ever put his hopes, his dreams on a child who would probably only smash them all in the end anyway.

He opened his eyes and stood from the sofa, his thoughts drifting from Maggie to her mother. Who would have thought that in just a little over a week a woman would have managed to get so deep beneath his skin?

Kurt's woman. The words played through his head, taunting him. Breanna had fallen in love and married a man who had been bigger than life, filled with energy and excitement.

Adam couldn't compete with that. He was an accountant, a man who always played it safe, a man who always did the right thing. And the right thing now was to leave Cherokee Corners, leave Breanna and Maggie to their wonderful family, their rich culture and the full life they had here without him.

It took Breanna a very long time to fall asleep that night. She stood at her bedroom window in the dark, watching the moonlight play on the leaves of the big oak tree just outside.

Thoughts of Adam filled her heart, filled her soul as no man had ever done before. How was it possible in just the brief time she'd known him? And how was it possible that she felt as if she'd known him forever?

Her physical attraction to him had been instantaneous and her trust in him, in his good character had quickly followed.

Sharing the day with him at the Cultural Center had held its own special brand of magic. He'd seemed eager to learn about her people, their customs and beliefs and unlike with Kurt, she'd wanted to share it all with Adam.

She'd watched him interacting with people and found herself admiring his easygoing nature, his openness and friendliness that drew others to him.

It had been while watching Adam interact with Maggie that she had decided to trust his judgment about Anita and Edward Randolf. A man as naturally gentle as Adam, a man as affectionate with Maggie wouldn't do anything to put her at risk either physically or emotionally. She trusted Adam enough to believe his sentiments about his aunt and uncle.

She turned away from the window and got into bed, wondering how long it would be before the Randolfs contacted her. Had Adam already called them to tell them the news? Maggie would never know her father, but hopefully she would know the love of his parents.

She'd known in telling Adam that he could tell Kurt's parents she was effectively sending him on his way. It was the final loose end he had to clean up. Now there was nothing to keep him from getting back to his real life.

She'd known all along there would be a goodbye. She just hadn't realized how difficult that goodbye would be. Was he packing already? Maybe preparing to leave with dawn's light? A sharp pain pierced through her.

She'd told him she didn't want a relationship, but she hadn't anticipated falling in love with him. She'd thought she could handle a casual affair with him and not be touched emotionally. She'd been so wrong.

It had been ill-fated from the beginning. He had come to Cherokee Corners to clean up a mess. She and her child had been that mess. His job was done here and it was time to say goodbye.

She was surprised by the tears that burned hot behind her eyes…unexpected tears, unwanted tears. She had sworn to herself that a man would never make her cry again. But she hadn't counted on Adam and the tears that she shed were for the life they'd never have together, the dreams she'd never build with him.

She'd thought she was just on the verge of falling in love with him, but she'd been wrong. She'd fallen head over heels in love and the ache of knowing there was no happy ending for them ripped her up inside.

She fell asleep with tears still staining her cheeks, and awoke with the sun shining full in her face. When she looked at the clock she was surprised to realize it was almost nine. It was unusual for Maggie not to awaken her long before now.

A peek into Maggie's room showed the little girl still sleeping soundly. Apparently the festivities the day before had exhausted her.

Breanna pulled on a robe and went downstairs, eager for coffee. She studiously refused to think about Adam Spencer, but she did notice his car was still in the driveway of the cottage.

No more tears, she told herself firmly. Her life would return to exactly the way it had been before she'd met Adam Spencer. She had a job she loved, a child she adored, a terrific nanny and a wonderful family.

She'd just sat down at the table and started sipping her first cup of coffee when the child she adored bounded down the stairs.

"Good morning, sweetness," she said.

"Hi, Mommy. I'm hungry." Maggie slid into the chair across from Breanna and smiled winsomely. "I think it's a nice morning for pancakes."

"You do?" Breanna smiled at her daughter. "And who do you think should make these pancakes?"

"Maybe you and me?" Maggie looked at her pleadingly.

This is what's important, Breanna thought moments later as Maggie stirred the batter for the pancakes and chattered like a magpie. This was all that was important in life, her daughter. Not a man, not a relationship, not love or sex, just quality time spent with Maggie.

They ate breakfast, then while Breanna was cleaning up the kitchen, Maggie ran upstairs, dressed for the day, then came back down stairs with a blanket in hand and announced she intended to play house in the front yard.

"But it won't be the same without Mr. Bear," she said.

Breanna leaned down and gave her a hug. "I'll call Uncle Clay and ask him if later today we can go pick up Mr. Bear."

"Since I don't have Mr. Bear, would you play house with me?"

"Sure, just let me get dressed and I'll be happy to play with you."

It was a perfect way to spend some of the time on her day off, playing house with her daughter, Breanna thought moments later as she changed from her nightshirt and robe into a pair of shorts and an old T-shirt.

As she brushed her hair and carefully braided it into one thick braid down her back, she heard Maggie running up and down the stairs and knew she was taking half her stuffed animals and toys out to the blanket on the front lawn.

Before she went back downstairs, she placed a quick call to Clay and made arrangements to meet him at his lab at two that afternoon to pick up Mr. Bear. She should have gotten the bear the day after Clay had told her it had yielded no information. Mr. Bear had been with Maggie since the day she'd been born.

She went back down the stairs, poured herself a

fresh cup of coffee and was about to go outside when the phone rang.

"Your father is annoyed with me," Rita said the moment Breanna said hello.

"What is it this time?" She walked through the kitchen to the living room window and peered out to see Maggie busily setting up her "house" on the blanket.

"He wants to take me on a cruise."

Breanna laughed and walked back into the kitchen for her coffee. "I wish somebody would get annoyed with me and offer to take me on a cruise."

"He's annoyed because I don't want to go," Rita exclaimed.

"Why ever not?"

"He wants to go next month. He knows how busy I am in the summer months at the Cultural Center."

"Mother, I'm sure somebody could take over your duties there for a week or two." Breanna shut off the coffeepot and emptied the last of the coffee down the sink.

"That's beside the point," Rita replied indignantly. "The fact that he would even think about going then shows his utter lack of respect for my work."

"I'm sure you two will work it out," Breanna replied. "I've got to go, Mom. Maggie's waiting for me. We're going to play house."

"All right. Give her a kiss for me and tell her I'll do my best not to kill her grandfather."

Breanna laughed. "I'll give her a kiss for you." The two women said their goodbyes and hung up.

Breanna walked through the living room and out the front door, surprised to see that Maggie wasn't in the front yard. Thinking she must have come back into the house while Breanna had been on the phone, she went back inside and stood at the bottom of the stairs.

"Maggie, I'm ready to play. There's no need to bring out everything you own."

She waited a moment, then two for a reply. When there was none, she walked up two of the stairs. "Hey, kiddo, what are you doing up there?"

Still no reply. Breanna walked up the stairs and peered into her daughter's bedroom. There was no sign of Maggie.

I must have missed her outside, Breanna thought as she ran lightly back down the stairs and out the front door. But there was still no Maggie anywhere visible in the front yard.

"Maggie!" Breanna yelled as she started around the side of the house, thinking perhaps her daughter had gone around to the back for something.

She ignored the quickened pace of her heart, telling herself not to panic. Maggie was probably playing with her, giggling as Breanna walked within inches of her hiding place.

"Maggie, answer me! Where are you? Honey, you're scaring me. Come on and let's play house."

Breanna's heartbeat boomed like thunder in her chest as there was still no sound of Maggie's voice, no sight of her anywhere.

She ran back to the front of the house, a sense of panic welling up inside her. The blanket was there, the stuffed animals were there, the little plastic dishes were there, but where was Maggie?

Dear God…where was Maggie?

Chapter 13

Adam had slept late, having tossed and turned all night until dawn streaked the sky.

He got out of bed, showered and dressed and was seated at the table having his first cup of coffee for the day when somebody banged on the front door.

He hurried to the door and peeked through the peephole. It was Breanna. He pulled the door open and was about to greet her when she slammed her fists against his chest. "Where is she?" she demanded. "Where have they taken her?" She drew back her fists, her eyes wild. He anticipated her hitting him again and grabbed her by the wrists.

"Calm down," he exclaimed.

She struggled to get free of his grip. "Don't tell me to calm down. Where's my daughter…where have they taken her?"

"Where has who taken her?" Adam asked in bewilderment.

"The Randolfs," she practically screamed as she managed to wrench her wrists from his hold.

"Breanna, what in the hell are you talking about? I haven't even told my aunt and uncle about Maggie yet."

"Oh…I thought…maybe…" Her eyes were stark with panic. "I can't find her, Adam." She grabbed one of his hands and squeezed tightly. "I can't find Maggie."

Quickly, in halting words, she explained to him that the last time she'd seen Maggie, she'd been in the front yard setting up for a game of house.

"Come on, let's go look again," Adam said, refusing to panic until there was a good reason.

Maggie wasn't in the front yard as they hurried to the house. "Maybe she's hiding," he suggested. "Why don't we check out the house first. You take the downstairs and I'll take the upstairs."

As he took the stairs two at a time he could hear Breanna calling for her daughter in the downstairs. There were four bedrooms in the upstairs of the old Victorian. He checked Maggie's first, peeking into the closet, under the bed, anywhere a little girl could squeeze into.

From Maggie's room he went into Breanna's, trying not to remember the near-love scene that had taken place on her bed the day he'd plugged in her caller ID box. He also checked in the closet and beneath the bed, all the while softly calling the little girl's name.

He was trying not to panic, trying not to feed off the sheer panic he heard in Breanna's voice as she checked the downstairs.

Children hid from their parents all the time, didn't they? Hide-and-seek was one of their favorite games.

From Breanna's room he went down the hall to a bathroom, then into the next bedroom which apparently belonged to Rachel. Across from Rachel's room was a spare room containing only a couple of boxes of what appeared to be Christmas decorations.

He hurried back downstairs and met Breanna in the foyer. Never in his life had he seen such desperation on anyone's face. Her eyes were black with it and her entire body appeared to be trembling.

"Come on, let's look outside again," he said, trying to remain as calm as possible. "Would she have left the yard?" he asked as they stepped outside.

"No. She knows never to leave the yard," she replied emphatically. "It's one of our rules and Maggie doesn't break the rules." She gazed at him beseechingly, as if pleading with him to make everything all right.

"Check under your porch and mine," he instructed. "I'll go around the back and check my shed. Maybe she decided to do a bit of exploring."

She nodded, as if relieved to have something, anything constructive to do. Adam hurried to his backyard, his heart double-timing it with anxiety.

Maybe she decided to check out the shed and something fell and hit her on the head. The shed was nothing more than an accident waiting to happen.

Where else could she be? What could have happened to her? Alyssa's words of foreboding echoed sharply in his brain as he ran toward the old ramshackle shed behind his house.

She didn't break the rules, Breanna had said, but as he checked the shed and found no sign of Maggie, he told himself that even the best of kids occasionally broke the rules.

He hurried back to Breanna in the front yard. The expression of hope that lit her features fell as she saw him returning empty-handed. It broke his heart.

"Oh God, Adam, where is she?"

He frowned and drew a hand through his hair in frustration. "Maybe she saw a cat running by, or a dog...or even a squirrel and decided to run after it. A five-year-old wouldn't have to get far from home to be utterly lost."

Again a shine of hope lightened the darkness of her eyes. "You're right, that's probably it. She loves animals. And just because she's never broken the rule before doesn't mean she didn't now."

"I'll do a quick canvas of the neighborhood," Adam said. "Maybe one of the neighbors saw her go by."

"I'll go, too. We can find her twice as fast with both of us looking."

He shook his head. "No, you need to stay here. She may come back, or maybe she'll stop at somebody's house and tell them she's lost. You need to stay here and by the phone."

He knew she'd rather be out actively searching instead of passively sitting and waiting and he reached out and squeezed her icy cold, trembling hand. "If I find her, I'll call you immediately."

He didn't wait for her reply, but dropped her hand and hurried off. There was a bad feeling in his gut...a sickening feeling that he knew wouldn't go away until Maggie was found safe and sound.

Alyssa's feeling of danger to someone she loved echoed again through his head as the thought of the disturbing phone calls Breanna had received joined in.

He hoped neither had anything to do with Maggie's disappearance. He desperately hoped that it was as he'd speculated...Maggie had left the yard and was too young to find her way back home.

He had no idea which direction to pick and so arbitrarily went in the direction the three of them had walked the night they'd gone into town for ice cream.

The first two houses he stopped at his knocks on the doors went unanswered and he assumed nobody was home. In the driveway of the third house, a teenage boy was washing his car. He told Adam he hadn't seen a little girl pass by, but he'd only been outside for about ten minutes. Adam hurried on.

Two doors up from where the boy was outside, Adam saw an older man trimming bushes in his front yard. "Have you seen a little girl?" Adam asked.

"You got one that's lost?" The old man put down his clippers and approached where Adam stood on the sidewalk.

"We've got one we can't find," Adam replied.

"Well, I've been out here working in the yard all morning and I haven't seen any little ones around, but good luck finding her."

They needed more than good luck, Adam thought as he hurried back the way he had come. There was no point going any farther in this direction if the old man had been in his yard all morning and hadn't seen Maggie pass by.

As Breanna's place came back into view, he saw her seated on the front porch and knew the phone was clutched tightly in her hand.

She stood as she saw him, her body taut with tension. He heard the deep, wrenching sob that broke loose from her. She ran to him, reaching him on the sidewalk and instantly he wrapped his arms around her and pulled her tight against his chest.

Her familiar scent wrapped around him, but this time it was tinged with the odor of fear. "We'll find her," he whispered into her ear. "But I think it's time we call the police."

"I already have," she replied, then drew a deep breath and stepped out of his embrace. "Somebody should be here any minute." She offered him a smile that was aching in its desperation. "I'm sure everything is going to be just fine." She turned to walk back to the porch and wait for the authorities.

Adam was about to follow her, but stopped, frozen in place as his gaze drifted down and locked on something in the grass by the curb.

It was something pink…something hot pink. Without taking a single step closer he knew what it was. An icy chill took possession of his blood.

Thunder. The pink plastic horse that Maggie wore around her neck was no longer around her neck, but rather in the grass by the curb.

On wooden legs he stepped forward until he was close enough to see that was, indeed, what it was. He started to bend down to retrieve it, but quickly changed his mind, knowing it was important for the police to see exactly where it was…right next to the street curb…right next to where a car might have parked.

He hurried toward Breanna, deciding not to mention it to her. Time enough for that when the police arrived. Adam didn't have to be a psychic to know that things looked bad…things looked very bad.

* * *

Adam had just joined her on the porch when the
first patrol car pulled into the driveway behind
Breanna's car. For Breanna, time had lost all meaning. One minute was like the next...an agony of uncertainty without her precious daughter.

Before she could rise to greet the officers who
climbed out of the patrol car, Adam hurried to meet
them. She saw him pointing to something in the grass
and she raced toward them.

When she saw what Adam had pointed at, a cry
tore from her throat as agony ripped through her. Before anyone could stop her, she reached down and
grabbed the plastic charm. The chain was still on it,
broken in half as if yanked off forcefully.

She was a cop and the implication of the broken
chain along with where it had been found wasn't lost
on her. Maggie wasn't just missing. She wasn't going
to be found in the neighborhood. Somebody had taken
her against her will and put her in a car and driven
off.

"Don't jump to conclusions," Ben Larsen, one of
the responding officers, said as if he could read her
mind. "We don't know how that necklace got there."
He held out his hand for the necklace.

Breanna dropped it in his palm, although her instinct was to hold tight to it...and keep holding it until
Maggie was back safe and sound in her arms.

She didn't realize she was crying until she tasted
the salt of tears in her mouth, then she quickly swiped
her tears. Now was not the time to cry. They had to
find Maggie.

Adam placed an arm around her. She wanted to

lean in to him, to give way to the sheer terror that gripped her heart. But she couldn't. Not now.

"I'll call for a couple more cars," Ben said. "We'll start canvassing the neighborhood. Breanna, what was your daughter wearing when you last saw her?"

Wearing? As a cop, she knew how important it was that all the officers get an accurate description of Maggie, but for a moment her mind faltered as she tried to think of what Maggie had put on that morning.

Had she worn her pink shorts set, or a pair of jeans and a T-shirt? Why, oh why hadn't she paid more attention? Pink, she remembered now. Maggie had spilled some syrup on her shirt and Breanna had washed it off.

"Pink shorts and a pink flowered short-sleeved blouse," she said.

Ben nodded and got on his radio. Fred Macon, his partner eyed Breanna sympathetically. "We'll find her, Bree," he said. His gaze turned apologetic as he drew a pad and pen from his pocket. "You know there's certain questions I need to ask you. But first," he looked at Adam, "could I get your name, sir?"

"He's Adam Spencer. He lives next door." Breanna gestured toward the cottage.

"Could I speak with you, Mr. Spencer, alone?" Fred asked.

"Okay," Adam agreed.

"That isn't necessary, Fred," Breanna said impatiently. "He had nothing to do with Maggie's disappearance. I don't beat my child so he wouldn't have seen anything or heard anything that might lead you to believe I harmed my child. Maggie doesn't run away and Adam isn't the neighborhood pedophile." The words tumbled from her in frustration.

She knew the game, but they didn't have time to play this one by the book, knew that precious minutes were slipping away with unnecessary questions.

Before Fred could reply, another patrol car squealed to a halt before the house and Savannah got out of the driver's side. The sight of her sister set off her tears again and she ran to Savannah with arms outstretched. A million times in the past the two sisters had found solace in each other's arms.

It had been Savannah who had been at her side when she'd given birth to Maggie, Savannah who had bought the child her first teddy bear, the favorite stuffed animal, Mr. Bear.

But Savannah's arms held no comfort this time. Just as Breanna knew the night Savannah's husband had died, Breanna's hug had done nothing to ease Savannah's heartbreak.

Savannah hugged her tight for a long moment, then released her and held her at arm's length. "Tell me what's going on," she said, her lovely features taut with strain.

Quickly Breanna filled her in, the darkness in Savannah's eyes mirroring the darkness in Breanna's heart. "Then let's get busy and find her," Savannah said.

Within minutes two more patrol cars had arrived and officers were out canvassing the neighborhood, talking to people, trying to learn if anyone had seen little Maggie.

Glen Cleberg, chief of police, arrived and led Breanna and Adam into her living room where he made her recount the morning activities yet another time.

"Glen, for God's sake. We've got to do something," she exclaimed, knowing that if somebody had abducted Maggie, the first couple of hours were critical. Already the officers had grilled her on Maggie's friends and acquaintances and asked about Kurt.

"We're doing everything we can," he replied. "What I need from you now is a recent photo of Maggie. We'll put an amber alert into motion immediately. We'll have the whole city looking for her."

His words should have brought her some sort of comfort, but Breanna was beyond comfort. She felt curiously numb, but knew that when the numbness wore off she would fall into an abyss of darkness and terror that would consume her. The terror already whispered to her, beckoning her to fall into its icy grip, but she fought against it.

She got her purse and pulled out her wallet. Inside was an identification card with a photo of Maggie. She held it for a moment, staring down at the beloved face of her daughter until her vision blurred with tears.

In the photo Maggie was wearing a T-shirt with a happy face on the front. Her smile was full, her soft gray eyes twinkling with good humor.

Breanna remembered the day they had gotten the identification card done. An organization devoted to child safety had set up in a chain discount store and Maggie, who loved to have her photo taken, had been delighted to go through the process. They'd been shopping for a night-light that day for her room.

"Bree." Adam's voice was a soft intrusion into her

memory. She looked up to see him watching her, his eyes filled with worry. Gently, he took the card from her and handed it to Glen.

"I'll see that copies of this are dispersed to the press," Glen said. "In the meantime, you stay here next to the phone. I'm having <u>Brutmeyer</u> hook up a recording device so if a ransom call comes in we'll be able to tape it."

A ransom. The word shot a gripping fear through Breanna. A ransom couldn't be made unless somebody had been kidnapped. Oh God, please don't let Maggie be kidnapped, she prayed.

"It's just a precaution," Glen said. "Of course, we're hoping she'll turn up safe and sound someplace in the neighborhood. Why don't you put on some coffee for the officers who are going to be here until we find her," he suggested.

She knew all about making coffee. It was what was suggested to the members of every victim's family during an investigation, an action that would keep them busy and out of the investigators' hair. She'd make coffee, but there was no way she was going to stay out of anyone's hair. She didn't intend to stand around and serve the officers as they drifted in and out of her kitchen.

She wasn't simply a citizen, a victim of crime. She was a cop and her daughter was missing and she intended to do what she did best...be a cop.

As the coffee brewed, Adam hovered nearby, as if at any moment he expected her to collapse. "I'm not going to pull my hair out or faint from stress," she exclaimed to him.

"I know that."

"Well, you're hovering," she said with a touch of

irritation. Then she looked…really looked at his face. His features were drawn with worry and his eyes radiated a whisper of fear. It hit her hard, in the center of her heart. He cared about Maggie.

"I'm sorry," he said, averting his gaze from hers. "I didn't mean to make you uncomfortable. I just…I just feel so damned useless." His sharp voice spoke of frustration.

She walked over and stood mere inches in front of him. She placed her hands on either side of his face, feeling the faint burr of whiskers on his jaw. "You love her, too, don't you Adam? It's impossible to know Maggie and not love her."

His gaze met hers again and in the dark blue depths of his eyes she saw the answer to her question. "Yes, I love her." The words sounded as if they were ripped reluctantly from someplace deep inside him.

She leaned into him then and allowed herself the weakness of weeping against his chest. He held on to her as if they were both standing on the edge of a dangerous precipice and he was the anchor keeping them safe.

"Breanna?"

Reluctantly she left Adam's arms and swiped at her hot tears as Ben Larsen stepped into the kitchen. "Any news?" she asked hopefully. The young officer's expression answered her question.

"Your parents are outside and Clay has arrived."

Together Adam and Breanna followed Ben to the front porch. Breanna watched her brother taping off the entire front yard with bright yellow tape. The sight of the familiar crime scene tape sent a frigid chill up her spine.

Her parents and Alyssa stood in the driveway, each

of their faces reflecting the horror that Breanna felt. She walked over to fill them in on what was going on.

Thomas placed an arm around Rita's shoulder as silent tears oozed from her eyes. Through the veil of tears, a steely strength shone through. "You tell us what to do and we'll do it."

"Maybe you could go inside and see that the men who are helping have something to eat and coffee to drink," Breanna suggested.

Rita nodded, then reached out and hugged Breanna tightly. "We'll find our little doe."

As her parents went into the house, Breanna turned to Alyssa, whose face radiated a tortured pain. "Oh, Bree. I'm so sorry. I wish I'd known more...could have warned you...I knew something bad was coming...but I never dreamed it would be Maggie."

"Shhh." Breanna stilled her by pulling her into a hug. "Nothing bad is going to happen. We're going to find Maggie safe and sound." She said the words fervently, desperately wanting to believe them.

"If only I'd seen something that might help." This was the torture of the visions Alyssa suffered and Breanna knew what her cousin was feeling, that somehow she should be able to help, that the damned visions should come when they were most needed.

"Alyssa, if I even think that you're feeling guilty, it will only makes things worse. Now, go help Mom and Dad in the kitchen." She squeezed her cousin's hand and forced a smile. "It's going to be all right...truly."

"Keep those people off the lawn." Clay's stern voice rang in the air as he pointed to a couple of neighbors who were obviously curious about the commotion. Two uniformed cops hurried to comply with his order.

"He doesn't want the scene contaminated," she said to Adam who had suddenly appeared at her side. "Now his team will search by grids, looking for anything that might be a clue. It might be a footprint…or a discarded piece of chewing gum. He'll take her blanket and all the items she was playing with to the lab and check them for hairs and fibers, for a trace of anything somebody might have left behind."

She knew she was rambling and her gaze lingered on the pink blanket on the grass. Maggie…her heart cried out. Maggie, where are you? Hang on, baby. Please hang on because I can't imagine my life without you in it.

"Breanna." Adam's sharp voice pulled her from the edge of madness. She looked at him blankly. "There's nothing you can do out here. Let's go back inside and let Clay and his people do their jobs. They want you in there to answer the phone. People have started calling and you need to keep the line clear."

The numbness was wearing off. She looked at her clock, shocked to see that it was almost two in the afternoon. Maggie had been missing for at least three hours. Three hours. Her mind screamed in protest.

She allowed Adam to lead her into the house and to the sofa. Somebody had turned on the television and she sat down next to the phone that now had a recording device on it. The technician explained to her which button to push before she answered, then left her and Adam alone.

When the phone rang it jangled every nerve in her body, but it was just a neighbor wondering what was going on. The next five phone calls were all the same, concerned friends and acquaintances wondering what was happening. Breanna got them off the line as quickly as possible.

It wasn't until she saw the amber alert on the television screen that the stark reality struck and the last of her numbness shot away. The amber alert was an immediate official response when a child went missing.

Maggie's picture was in a small box at the bottom of the screen, following by a trailer that gave her name and age and what she was wearing. Breanna read it as Adam grabbed her hand tightly. "Last seen playing in her front yard," the trailer read.

"Last seen." Breanna spoke the words aloud. "Those are words a parent should never have to see or hear about their child. Last seen." She covered her face with her hands and wept, no longer feeling like a cop, but rather simply a mother in the worst kind of pain imaginable.

Adam held her as she wept tears of fright, tears of uncertainty. Her arms ached with the need to hold Maggie. She needed to smell the scent of her baby girl, feel her wiggly warmth in her arms. She needed to hear Maggie's laughter filling a room, see those beautiful baby eyes that always held a magical sparkle.

The phone rang yet again and she jerked away from Adam's embrace. She punched the button to begin the recorder, then picked up the phone and breathed an exhausted hello.

The music started immediately, the woman singing the familiar lullaby. Breanna's gaze shot to Adam's, panicked. He quickly motioned to one of the officers as Breanna placed the call on speakerphone.

The lullaby filled the living room, the woman's voice sweet and soft. When the music stopped, there was a pregnant silence. "Hello? Who's there?" Breanna asked, wishing she could crawl through the line and discover who was on the other end.

"Now we're even," a male voice said. Deep, dark laughter filled the line, then silence.

Chapter 14

"The call came from 555-2314," the technician said as he punched things into a laptop computer.

"Come on, Tom. Where's the phone," Cleberg asked.

"Wait...I got it...Tenth and Main. It's a pay phone."

Before the words were out of his mouth, Breanna was out the door. She surprised Adam by running toward his place, then he realized what she was doing. Her car was blocked in by other cars. His was not.

"Breanna," Cleberg shouted after them. "Officer James! You are not working this case as a cop. Get back here."

She ignored him and instead got into the driver seat of his car. "Give me your keys," she said, her eyes wild with urgency.

"I'm not letting you drive anywhere," he protested. "You want to get to that phone, you let me drive.'' She sighed in frustration, but moved over to the passenger side. He slid in and pulled out of his driveway with a squeal of his tires and pointed the car in the direction of Main Street.

He looked in his rearview mirror and saw two patrol cars behind him, their lights flashing and sirens wailing. ''Ignore them,'' she said tersely.

''You really don't think anyone is going to be at that phone, do you?'' he asked. She didn't reply and he realized then that her hope was irrational, the hope of a mother clinging to straws.

Adam stepped on the gas, driven by his own irrational hope that maybe the bastard who took Maggie had stopped to make the call and his car had broken down, or he'd parked illegally and somebody was towing the car away, Maggie sleeping comfortably in the backseat.

Funny, how love could mess with your mind. Love. Despite his desire never to love a child who could break his heart, somehow Maggie had managed to crawl beneath the defenses he'd tried to erect. He loved her, and with every minute that passed his heart was breaking in a way he hadn't thought possible. He couldn't imagine the pain Breanna must be feeling.

She pointed just ahead of him. ''There.''

The phone booth was an old-fashioned kind that was rarely seen anymore. Adam squealed to a halt in front of it as Breanna jumped out of the passenger side and looked around, her gaze sweeping from side to side as she checked out the area. ''Don't touch the phone,'' she instructed Adam, although he had no intention of doing so.

The other officers surrounded the phone booth with the intention of keeping out everyone. Adam figured eventually one of the crime scene people would be out here to check for evidence...something...anything the perpetrator might have left behind.

"I knew there wouldn't be anything here," she said bitterly. "But I couldn't take just sitting in that house another minute."

He understood her need to do something, but what could they do? They had nothing but a disembodied voice on the phone to go on.

"Breanna, the officers will keep an eye on things here. We really need to go back to the house," he said.

She nodded, her shoulders slumping forward. Without any argument, she got back into his car. They drove in silence and Adam tried to think of something...anything to say that might help. But he recognized that words held no power to soothe in a situation like this.

She'd already amazed him with her strength. The tears she'd shed had been brief and instead what he felt now from her was a restless energy to do something...anything to help.

When they returned to the house, Clay was gone, along with the blanket and the items that had been on the front lawn. The other two crime scene investigators who worked with Clay were still combing the front yard, looking for clues.

"Dammit, Breanna," Glen Cleberg met them at the front door. "I know how you feel, but you can't go off all half-cocked like that."

"You don't know how I feel," she replied. "Somebody has taken my daughter and I'm not about to sit here twiddling my thumbs. I'm a cop, Glen, and if you keep me out of the loop I'll go crazy. And now I'm going upstairs.'' She shot Adam a pointed look. ''I'd like a few minutes alone.''

Without waiting for a reply, she climbed the staircase and disappeared into her bedroom.

Glen Cleberg looked at Adam and shook his head. ''This entire investigation has been taken over by the James family and by rights none of them should be working the case. But they're stubborn, and all three of them are the best I've got on the force.'' He rubbed a hand over his meaty jaw. ''I never thought I'd see the day that children couldn't play in their own front yards here in Cherokee Corners.''

''It only takes one bad person in a town to make everyone afraid,'' Adam replied, his gaze going up the staircase, his thoughts on Breanna. What must be going through her mind? How much uncertainty could one mother stand?

''I've got to say, Mr. Spencer, I got a bad feeling about this one. We got nothing to go on. So far nobody has turned up a witness who saw a suspicious car around here, or anyone who has seen little Maggie.''

''Maybe Clay will find something on the blanket that will help,'' Adam offered.

''Maybe,'' Glen replied, but he didn't sound too hopeful. ''But only if the perp was on that blanket. If he grabbed her out by the curb where her necklace was found, then he won't find squat.''

''What about Michael Rivers?'' Adam asked.

''We already checked him out. He's been at work all day. I talked to his boss and had one of the local cops check it out. I wish to hell it would have been that easy.''

Without waiting for Adam's reply, the chief of police turned and disappeared into the kitchen. The phone rang and the technician answered. It was obvious by his words that it was yet another acquaintance wanting information.

Adam sat in a chair in the living room, feeling more helpless than he ever had in his life. He'd just sat down when Alyssa came out of the kitchen, something clutched in her hand.

He stood. "What's up?" he asked.

She held out a photo of Maggie. "I'm going to get flyers made and see that they get distributed all over town."

He could see the remnants of tears, the red-rimmed lids around eyes that held fear...pain...and guilt. "Alyssa, there's nothing you could have done to prevent this."

"Logically, I know that," she replied. "But emotionally I keep wondering if there is something I missed...some vision that I didn't see clearly that might help." Tears sparked in her eyes, but she drew a deep breath and straightened her shoulders. "I've got to go. At least I have something constructive to do."

The minutes ticked by, broken only by officers coming in and out of the house and the ringing of the telephone. Adam sat in the living room thinking of Breanna...thinking of Maggie.

Maggie, who had wanted him to tell her he was proud of her because that's what daddies did. Maggie, who had told him if he ever needed a temporary pretend daughter, he could borrow her.

And now she was missing...apparently taken by a stranger and the pain that pierced his heart was all encompassing. That's why he hadn't wanted to have children...because they always broke your heart.

He sat on the sofa until the scent of hamburgers cooking filled the air. Rita must be cooking up something for everyone. Breanna had eaten no lunch. He needed to get her back down here to eat something.

He climbed the stairs, afraid of intruding, yet unable to spend another minute without seeing if Breanna was okay. Of course she's not okay, his brain screamed at him. She may never be okay again.

She wasn't in her bedroom, although he was surprised to see the clothes that she'd been wearing on the bed. He peeked into Maggie's room and there she was, sitting on the edge of Maggie's bed.

It was the first time he'd seen her in her official uniform. The khaki shirt and slacks should have looked masculine on her, but instead seemed to emphasize her utter femininity.

She looked up at him as he entered. Her eyes were tearless, but hollow. "It's going to be dark soon," she said. She didn't look at him, but rather stared down at the stuffed rabbit she held on her lap. "I hope she got to eat lunch...or at least will get dinner. She gets so cranky when she's hungry."

Adam said nothing and she stroked the rabbit fur and continued. "When she gets back, I'll take her out for chicken nuggets. That's her favorite. I worry sometimes because that's all she ever orders when we go out. She never tries anything new. But when she gets back I'll let her order all the chicken nuggets she wants and I won't say a word."

He leaned against the doorjamb, letting her ramble, knowing this moment would haunt him for years to come. "She's afraid of the dark. That's why she al-

ways sleeps with a night-light.'' For the first time
since he'd entered the room she looked up at him.
''We have to find her before dark.''

He nodded, his chest so tight he couldn't speak,
couldn't move. He wanted to wrap her in his arms
and never let her go, wanted to hunt down whomever
had caused this pain and kill him. Adam wasn't normally a violent man, but a blood thirst filled him as
he gazed at Breanna.

''Your mother is cooking some dinner.'' He finally
found his voice. ''Why don't you come down and get
something to eat?''

She shook her head negatively. ''I'm not hungry.''

He didn't press the issue, had known before he
spoke that food for herself would be the last thing on
her mind. Her cell phone rang and she leaned over
and picked it up from Maggie's nightstand.

''James,'' she said as she answered. ''Yes, Clay.''
She stood and her tension filled the room. ''Yes...
okay...got it. And Clay...thanks.'' She clicked off and
looked at Adam. ''He checked the blanket and found
several things. Dirt...grass stain...Maggie's hair...just
what you'd expect to find on a blanket where a little
girl played. But, he also found a bit of concrete, some
tar and several feline hairs.''

She frowned. ''Feline hair...cat hair,'' she said
softly, more to herself than to him. Her eyes flashed
to his, wide with shock. ''I think I know who has
Maggie.'' She ran past him and down the stairs. He
hurried after her, his heart racing as he wondered why
cat hair had given her a name?

''Turn left here,'' Maggie instructed Adam. She
was horribly afraid she might be wrong and equally

horrified that she might be right. They'd left the house without anyone knowing where they were going. She knew Glen would pop a cork if he knew what she suspected and where she was going.

She also knew she was a fool for involving a civilian and going in without backup, but it couldn't be helped. Adam's car was easily accessible, hers was not. And she knew instinctively Adam would have never allowed her out of the house without him.

"You want to tell me where we're going?" Adam asked as they flew past the Cultural Center.

"My partner's place."

Adam eyed her sharply. "You think your partner has Maggie?"

"Yes...no...I don't know," she replied miserably. Abe, her heart cried. Is it possible? Could you really do something like this to me?

"What makes you think he'd do something like this?" he asked dubiously.

"He's retiring and the other day he was talking about how he wished he was going out with a bang...some big bust of some kind. Turn right up here at the intersection."

"I'm not sure I understand."

Breanna sighed in frustration. "I don't know, Adam. Maybe he took her and has her hidden away someplace, then he'll be the cop who finds her alive and well. It would be the perfect way to retire, as a hero."

"It sounds just a little bit crazy," Adam replied.

"I know." She chewed her bottom lip thoughtfully. And it would be out of character for the man who'd been her mentor, the man she'd trusted with her life more than once. She'd thought she'd known him, but she'd thought she'd known Kurt as well. Maybe she was just a bad judge of character.

"He also has a cat," she said, then added in desperation. "I can't not check him out, Adam. Even if I don't want to believe it."

She stared out the window, absently noting the thick stand of trees beyond which flowed the river. She touched the butt of her gun, hoping she wouldn't have to draw it against a fellow officer...against her own partner.

"Slow down," she said to Adam, her gaze locking on the copse of trees beyond which Abe's home stood. Dusk was beginning to fall, painting the trees with pale gold light and creating purple shadows amid the trees.

Was Maggie there? Dear God, she wanted her to be there and she didn't. She wanted her daughter more than anything, but she didn't want her partner to be the one responsible for her being missing.

"Turn right on the next dirt road. It will lead up to Abe's house." Adrenaline roared through her. "At least we aren't in a patrol car. He won't recognize this car."

"Why don't I go up and knock on the front door...kind of get a feel for things," Adam suggested as he slowed the car to a crawl.

"Absolutely not," she replied. "You stay in the car. I'll be in trouble for having you with me. The last thing I need is for you to get hurt."

Again he eyed her sharply, his blue gaze hard and cold. "If you think you're going in there alone, then you have another think coming." There was a stern, implacable edge to his voice she'd never heard before.

"Adam, please don't argue with me," she replied impatiently.

He stopped the car and turned in the seat. "I told you, Breanna. You are not going into that house alone. You'll have to shoot me to keep me in this car."

"All right, all right," she exclaimed, not wanting to take the time to fight with him. "The house is just around the corner. Let's go ahead and leave the car here and walk in."

Together they got out of the car and started walking down the dirt road that led to Abe's place. "Do you have a plan?" Adam asked quietly.

"None," she admitted. "I just intend to get inside and see if my daughter is there." She was grateful he didn't say anything more. She pulled her gun as the house came into view.

It was a small, two-bedroom cottage tucked amid the trees. Breanna had visited Abe here on many occasions. She'd eaten dinner with him, brought her daughter here to fish with Uncle Abe in the river that ran across the back of his property.

As she stared at the house, she reviewed the floor plan in her mind and tried to figure out the best way to approach. "I'm going straight in," she said aloud. "I'm just going to knock on the door and see what happens."

Adam simply nodded, apparently trusting her judgment. Drawing a deep breath, she started across the yard toward the front door. Adam walked next to her and strangely enough she felt as if he was all the backup she needed.

He exuded strength and energy and she knew he would have her back. He reached the front door before her and knocked. Even the sound of his fist on the wooden door sounded strong and capable.

They waited a moment or two for a reply and when there was none, Adam knocked again, this time more forcefully.

"I'm coming...hold your horses," Abe's voice came from inside the house.

Breanna tensed, knowing a confrontation was imminent. Abe opened the door and his face wreathed into a surprised smile. "Bree!" His smile faded as his gaze swept over her uniform. "Don't tell me I'm confused on my days and I'm supposed to be working."

"Can we come in, Abe?" she asked.

He frowned, obviously sensing the tension ripe in the air. "What's going on?" His fingers tightened on the door.

"We'd just like to come in and ask you a few questions," Adam said.

Abe eyed him suspiciously. "Who the hell are you, and hell no, you aren't coming in until somebody tells me what is going on."

Breanna's heart sank. As she saw the hurt confusion in Abe's eyes, she realized she was wrong. He'd never do anything to hurt her or Maggie. "Maggie's missing, Abe."

"Missing? What do you mean?" He looked at her with what appeared to be obvious confusion.

"She was in my front yard this morning and disappeared."

"What can I do to help? You need me at the station?"

Breanna hesitated. She had a feeling she was about to break an old man's heart. "No...we're just checking everything...everyone," she said vaguely.

Abe stared at her, then at Adam, then back again at her, the dawning of betrayal darkening his eyes. "You thought she might be here? You thought I had something to do with this?"

"There were cat hairs, Abe."

"Half the people in Cherokee Corners have cats." Abe threw open his door. "But don't take my word for it. Hell, Breanna, come in. Search my house. Do whatever you have to do, then get the hell out of here."

Breanna promptly burst into tears...because she knew she wouldn't find her daughter here...and because she'd just destroyed a relationship with a man she loved.

Chapter 15

Something had broken inside her. Although Abe had consoled her and insisted he wasn't angry with her, something had broken inside Breanna. It was as if all the grief she'd been holding in had surfaced and exploded into uncontrollable tears.

All the strength had seeped away from her and she didn't look like a cop anymore. She looked like a victim…slumped down in the seat…the inconsolable mother of a missing child. And darkness was falling.

Her wrenching sobs had finally ceased, leaving behind silent tears that continued to ooze down her cheeks as she stared out the passenger window.

Adam tried to think of something to say, anything to ease her pain. It filled the car, seeped into his pores and constricted his heart.

"It's got to be somebody I know," she finally said. The words surprised him. He'd thought she was lost in a sea of grief, but apparently she wasn't so lost that her brain wasn't working. "It isn't a stranger abduction." She sat up straighter in the seat and wiped her cheeks with the back of her hand. "Now we're even, that's what the voice said on the phone. Now we're even." She frowned thoughtfully.

"So, whose kid have you taken lately?" he asked half-jokingly.

"I don't know." She sat up even straighter in the seat. "Take me to the station, Adam. I need to pick something up."

He didn't ask questions, he merely did as she bid. When she reached the station house, he followed her inside. Fellow officers who offered their commiseration and aid greeted her.

They learned that while they'd been away from the house posters had been distributed and Jacob Kincaid had put up a ten thousand-dollar reward for information leading to the whereabouts of Maggie.

Breanna took in all this information stoically, then disappeared into a storage room and came out carrying a heavy box of files. Adam quickly took the box from her. "What's this?" he asked.

"All the cases I've worked on since I started in the department. I can't help but think that the man who has Maggie is hiding in these files." Her eyes burned with a renewed sense of purpose.

"Then let's get them back to your place and get busy on them."

Darkness had fallen completely as they once again parked in Adam's driveway, although every light in Breanna's house was on and several patrol cars were still parked out front.

The technician manning the phone greeted them

as they came back inside. "Anything?" Breanna asked him.

"Nothing."

They went into the kitchen to find the table laden with food. Several officers were filling plates and Breanna's mother was fussing over them like a mother hen. Her father was washing dishes, his face a stoic mask.

They both stopped what they were doing long enough to hug Breanna and again, the loyalty and love this family had for one another struck Adam.

"Neighbors have been bringing food," Rita said. Adam looked at the table where there appeared to be at least six different kinds of casseroles. The universal language of support and caring…the casserole.

Glen came into the kitchen, his face showing the wear of the day. "Where in the hell have you been?" he asked Breanna.

"It isn't important now," she replied.

He eyed the box Adam still held in his arms and frowned. "That looks like official police paperwork."

"It's my files, Chief," Breanna responded. "It's got to be a revenge thing. Maybe somebody we busted for drugs who lost their children to child welfare."

"Need some help going through them?" Glen asked. "I'll assign some men."

"I'll help," Savannah said from where she stood drying dishes.

At that moment Abe walked through the door. "Whatever it is you're talking about, I'll help." He looked at Breanna and even Adam could see the forgiveness in his eyes. "It's what a partner does."

Breanna's eyes moistened and she nodded.

They took the file box into the living room and got to work. Abe, Savannah, Thomas, Breanna, Adam and two officers each took a handful of the files and began reading the cases, hoping for something that might jump out at them.

Breanna had told them to look for cases where the person being arrested had been violent, where the arrest record showed a family and employment that might pertain to working with concrete and tar.

Adam made sure Breanna was facing away from the windows, not wanting her to see the deepening darkness of night. The television was on, although the sound was muted. But every time Adam looked at it he saw the amber alert running along the bottom of the screen. *Maggie James… Last seen…* The words haunted him.

Adam had never realized before that desperation had a scent, but it did and it filled the living room as everyone read file after file of arrests Breanna had made or had been a part of.

Breanna's reports were meticulous and neatly typed. It was slow, painstaking work. There was no place on the arrest sheets to indicate a family. The only way to discern that was to read the handwritten notes Breanna had taken and included with each of the arrest forms.

Reading file after file, Adam got a taste for what Breanna's work life was like and his admiration for her grew. It was obvious that she was good at what she did. He glanced at her, noting the dark circles beneath her eyes, the slump of her shoulders, the redness of her bottom lip where she had been chewing.

The minutes ticked by…minutes that left Maggie in the hands of a possibly revenge-crazed violent man. Adam couldn't forget the blow he'd received on his head and he hoped…prayed that the person who'd been capable of almost killing him with a brick wasn't the same person that held Maggie captive.

Was it already too late for little Maggie? Was she already lying in a ditch by the side of the road? He shook his head to dislodge such a horrendous thought, surprised to feel the burn of tears.

Not Maggie, he prayed. Please God, don't take Maggie…not now…not like this. He refocused on the files, wondering if they were merely spinning their wheels while a kidnapper took Maggie farther and farther away from Cherokee Corners.

It was midnight when they finally got through all the files. Each person had a small stack of possibilities for Breanna to look through.

Adam moved to sit next to her as she perused each file. He thought he could hear her heartbeat, feel it pounding as if her heart was in his chest. Find Maggie. Find Maggie. That was the rhythm of the beats— find Maggie…find Maggie.

"I don't know…I just don't know," she said softly. She looked at him, sheer agony reflected in her eyes. "There isn't enough information here. I don't remember half these cases. How am I supposed to do this? How am I supposed to find Maggie?"

He took the files from her and pulled her against him. "Calm down," he said as he stroked the length of her hair. "We'll find her. I swear, we'll find her." He prayed as he'd never prayed before, wishing he could do more for her.

She held tight to him, as if he were her lifeline to sanity. "It's so dark outside, Adam. It's so dark and she has to be so frightened. I can't stand the thought of her being afraid.'' She pulled away from him and reached for the files once again.

''Breanna, the phone calls started about ten days ago. Maybe you should take out all the old files, concentrate on the ones only a week or two before the calls started,'' he suggested.

She nodded and for the next few minutes weeded through the files until she had a total of ten in her lap. ''Now, take them one at a time and tell me about them.''

As she did, people drifted in and out of the living room, but nobody interrupted them by speaking. Adam listened as Breanna went through the cases. As she studied the files and spoke aloud, she seemed to remember more than she'd initially thought she would.

''This guy was a newlywed…two weeks married and he was trying to pay me for sex.'' She shook her head ruefully. ''He went a little crazy when we arrested him, screamed that we were ruining his marriage.''

''What happens when these men are arrested for soliciting prostitution?'' Adam asked.

''They're taken down to the station, fingerprinted and photographed, then given citations and they have to appear in court,'' Breanna explained. ''It's only a misdemeanor charge…really not a big deal.''

''Unless the little woman finds out and the marriage ends. His loss in exchange for yours?''

The slump disappeared from her shoulders as she sat up straighter on the sofa. ''How can we find out quickly if his wife left him?'' she asked.

''Easy enough. Give me your cell phone.'' There was a phone number on the arrest report and Adam quickly punched in it. "Could I speak to Mrs. Jennings?" he said into the receiver.

"What are you crazy? It's the middle of the damned night. She's sleeping. Who the hell is this?"

Adam hung up. "The little lady is in bed where she belongs."

Breanna dug out another file. They made eight phone calls before they hit one that counted. "May I speak to Mrs. Duncan?" Adam said into the cell phone to the gruff hello.

"She doesn't live here anymore. Who is this?"

Adam clicked off and turned to the young officer standing nearby. "We need to get some information on <u>Eddie Duncan,</u>" he said. "When he was arrested he said he was unemployed. We need to know immediately where he's working and the circumstances of his family life."

"I remember him," Breanna said as the officer hurried out of the room. "He was a tall, burly guy. He was another one that went crazy when we arrested him. Called me all kinds of names, told me if his wife found out his life would be ruined." Her eyes held an edge of wildness. "One ruined life for another? Now we're even?"

It seemed to take forever for the officer to return to the living room. "Eddie Duncan. Address is 5981 Cypress Road. Currently employed with the highway department. It will take a little longer to find out about his family status."

"Highway department. Tar...concrete...it's too coincidental to ignore." She jumped up from the sofa, but Adam grabbed her arm.

"You aren't doing this without official backup," he said firmly. "If this guy is the same one who hit

me in the head with that brick, then we know what
he's capable of. You don't want to put Maggie at risk
by going in alone.''

"You're right.'' She got on her cell phone and
called Cleberg who was at the station waiting for a
break in the case.

Within minutes a team of police officers was being
dispatched to check out the situation. Despite the fact
that Cleberg had put another officer in charge, everyone looked to Breanna for guidance, knowing she was
the one with the most at stake.

"His house is off the beaten track,'' Breanna said,
apparently knowing the area. "If it's the one I'm
thinking of, it's surrounded by trees. We'll park on
Highway Ten and go in on foot. Nobody approach
the house until I give the go-ahead.''

They all started out the door and Adam followed
Breanna. She stopped him at her car. "Adam, you
can't go.''

"You can't stop me. I can either ride with you or
I'll take my own car, but I'm going.'' She started to
protest, but he held up his hand. "You're wasting
precious time arguing a lost cause. You've forgotten…I love her, too.''

She gazed at him for a long moment, then nodded
and together they got into her car. "No sirens, no
lights,'' she said into her radio. These were the last
words spoken until they reached a section of dark,
deserted highway where the patrol cars gathered and
shut off their engines.

There were a total of six officers along with
Breanna and Adam. Adam could tell that the other
officers didn't approve of him being there, but Adam
wasn't leaving.

He had to be here, wanted to see firsthand if Breanna was reconnected with her daughter in a happy reunion. And he needed to be here in case the reunion wasn't joyous at all.

She thought she could smell Maggie's scent as they made their way through the thick woods toward Eddie Duncan's house. It was that special blend of childhood innocence, of sweet little girl and peach bubble bath.

Of course, it was impossible that she smelled it, but she needed to believe that she was close enough to Maggie to smell her, close enough to Maggie to save her.

She didn't even know if they were on the right trail. It was a hunch with little else behind it. It was possible that Eddie Duncan was a perfectly innocent man in all this and Maggie was a hundred miles from here.

She clutched her flashlight in her hand, although it wasn't turned on. Thankfully the moonlight cast down just enough illumination to allow them to move through the trees without artificial lighting.

Adam was right behind her and even though she knew his presence here wasn't right, she was grateful for it. He loved Maggie, too. She had to be here. Please let this hunch pay off, she prayed.

The house came into view, a small ranch. Lights shone from within, creating splashes of light on the overgrown lawn. Tall grass in the yard, dying flowers in a weed-choked flower bed gave the place an air of neglect.

She clicked on her radio. ''Check in,'' she said softly.

''Unit one in place.''

"Unit two ready."

"Three is ready, too."

The officers checked in, each from a different side of the house. Breanna and Adam remained hidden in the trees about twenty feet in front of the house.

"I'm going to check it out," she said. "Hold your positions." She turned to Adam. "You stay here. I'm just going to get closer and take a look around." She started to leave, but he grabbed her by the arm and stopped her.

"Be careful," he said, then leaned forward and covered her lips with his. It was a fast kiss, over almost before it had begun, but it warmed her as she left the copse of trees and moved closer to the house.

She avoided the pools of brightness from the lights inside the house and clung to the shadows as she made her way across the lawn.

When she reached the front of the house she paused. She couldn't take a chance on stepping onto the porch. The wood might creak or make noise that would draw the attention of whomever was in the house and she wasn't ready for that.

Instead she crept to the right side of the house where a window beckoned her to peek in. Cautiously, she raised her head just enough to look into the house. The window was in the kitchen, and the kitchen was empty of people. But her heart bucked and kicked in her chest as she saw the remnants of two tv dinners on the kitchen table. A beer can set next to one, a half-emptied glass of milk at the other.

The sight caused a wave of relief to wash over her that was almost overwhelming. If, indeed, Maggie was inside the house, then the odds were good she was still alive. Hopefully, that glass of milk and tv dinner indicated she was not only alive, but had been fed dinner as well.

But of course there were a million other scenarios. The extra dinner could have been for a friend of Eddie's, or a relative that lived with him. There was absolutely no guarantee that Maggie had sat in that kitchen chair.

She moved around to the back of the house where there were four windows. The first was dark, but as she peered in she realized there was a hall light on and she could see that this room was probably the master bedroom. The double bed was unmade and clothes were strewn over the floor. Several coffee cups sat on the nightstand, along with balled-up tissues and a lamp with a torn shade.

If nothing else, Eddie Duncan should be cited for being a slob, she thought as she moved to the next window, which was a bathroom.

The third window was another bedroom. She slapped a hand over her mouth to stop the cry that threatened to escape. It was a child's room. A rocking horse stood in one corner and toys littered the floor. But that wasn't what made her heart threaten to explode from her.

Maggie. She was on a single bed, her thumb in her mouth. She hadn't sucked her thumb for years and the sight of her baby made Breanna want to smash through the window, pluck her up off the bed and carry her to safety.

But it was her training that forced her to maintain control. She had no idea where in the house Eddie Duncan might be, knew that as long as Maggie was on the inside with him she was in imminent danger.

Was she okay? Was she sleeping? Breanna held her

breath, watching her baby. Had he drugged her…or were they already too late? Maggie stirred restlessly and a sigh of relief escaped Breanna.

As difficult as it was, she forced herself away from the window. The last window yielded a view of a spare bedroom packed with boxes and furniture.

As stealthily as possible, she made her way back to her original position. "She's there," she whispered to Adam. "And she's alive."

"Thank God," Adam murmured.

Breanna got on her radio and let the other officers know exactly where Maggie was located and the fact that it appeared through deduction that Eddie Duncan was probably located in the living room.

"I'm going to try to get Maggie through the bedroom window, but I need two of you here in the front to provide a distraction," she said.

Plans were made and once the officers were in their new positions, Breanna worked her way back around the house and once again to the window of the room where Maggie was sleeping. She radioed her men that she was in position, then waited, heart racing, palms sweaty and gun ready.

"Eddie Duncan…this is the Cherokee Corners Police Department." A voice boomed through the night. At the same time Breanna tapped on the window.

"Wake up," she whispered. Maggie had always slept hard.

"Come out with your hands up."

The male voice once again filled the air. She knocked on the window once again, nearly sobbing with relief as Maggie stirred. The thumb came out of her mouth as her eyes opened.

Breanna, afraid to knock again without knowing if

Eddie Duncan was at the front of the house or heading back to this room, willed her daughter to look at the window.

"Eddie Duncan. We have the house surrounded. Come out now with your hands over your head."

As the officers in the front of the house spoke over the bullhorn, Breanna reached up and tried to open the window. Although she didn't budge the locked window, her motion caught Maggie's attention. Breanna quickly signaled her daughter to keep quiet, then motioned for her to unlock the window. Seconds. It was all she needed to get Maggie to safety. Maggie's face was tearstained and her mouth formed the word *mommy* as she tried to unlock the window, but she didn't have the strength to switch the lever that would unlock the window.

A gunshot exploded and full-fledged panic slammed into Breanna. She had no idea who had fired, the police or Eddie, but she knew she had to get Maggie out the window now.

"Stand back," she yelled to her daughter. She took the butt end of her flashlight and crashed it into one of the little panes on the window. When the glass was out, she reached through, flipped the lock, then yanked the window open.

"Come on, baby," she cried as another gunshot resounded.

Maggie ran to the window and climbed over the sill and into her mother's arms. At that moment Breanna saw a shadow coming down the hallway toward the bedroom.

She set Maggie on the ground and gave her a shove. "Run, baby. Run as fast as you can for the trees."

Maggie didn't hesitate, but did as Breanna told her. Breanna sobbed in relief as she saw Maggie make the cover of the trees. Only then did she turn to run. She got only a few feet away from the house, then looked over her shoulder and froze. Eddie Duncan's face appeared in the open window, along with a pointed gun.

"You bitch!" he cried, his voice filled with venom.

Breanna knew he was going to shoot and she also knew at this close range he probably wouldn't miss. At least Maggie is safe, she thought as she fumbled for her own gun.

She heard Eddie's gun roar, as if from a million miles away, then she slammed to the ground, somebody else's body covering hers.

Another shot went off and Eddie screamed. It was the scream of the wounded and Breanna knew the officers had stormed the house.

Adam's bright blue eyes gazed at her. "You okay?" he asked, his voice sounding funny.

"You saved my life, but you're really heavy," she said.

"I always thought if I ever got shot, the bullet would probably come from your gun. Guess I was wrong." His eyes rolled up in the back of his head.

"Adam!" Breanna screamed as she struggled to get out from under his dead-heavy body. It was only when she got to her feet that she saw the blood gushing from the wound in his back. "Help me!" she cried, tears blurring her vision as she tried to staunch the bleeding.

"Hang on, Adam," she whispered. "Please, hang on." They had managed to save Maggie, but she'd never be able to forgive herself if the price she had to pay was Adam's life.

Chapter 16

It had been two weeks since Adam had taken a bullet in the back that had magically missed every vital organ except his spleen, which the doctors had removed.

He stood at the window of his hospital room, waiting for Breanna, who was coming to take him back to the cottage. He'd been champing at the bit for the past three days, eager to leave this medical institution behind.

For the past two weeks he'd been treated like a hero by everyone in town. It had been embarrassing as hell. He wasn't a hero, he was just an accountant who had somehow managed to get in way over his head.

Eddie Duncan's story had made the rounds. It had been a nurse who had told him that Eddie had been arrested by Breanna on a solicitation charge. His wife had found out and had left him, taking their four-year-old little girl with her. Neighbors said the little girl had been Eddie's life, and he went just a little bit crazy. According to neighbors, he'd stopped going to work, but had left the house at odd hours. He'd become secretive and furtive, and more than one source had indicated they thought he was drinking a lot.

He was in a bed in the same hospital where Adam was, being treated for a gunshot wound to the leg before standing trial on a number of charges.

Breanna and Maggie had come to visit Adam every day, as had most of her family members and half the town. His hospital room was overflowing with flower arrangements, their cloying fragrance filling the air. He'd told the nurses to disperse them around to other rooms.

"All set?"

He turned from the window to see Breanna. Her loveliness filled his heart, his soul and he knew it was time to leave Cherokee Corners behind. Today. When he arrived back at the cottage, he'd pack and leave. It was way past time for him to say his goodbyes.

"More than all set," he replied. "I hope I don't see another hospital room for years to come." He grabbed the duffel bag from the bed.

"Oh, no, you don't," a nurse said as she entered the room pushing a wheelchair. "All of our discharged patients get curbside transportation."

"That really isn't necessary," he protested.

"Yes, it is," she replied and took the duffel bag from him. "It's the rules." She looked at Breanna. "If you'd like to pull your car up in front, I'll push him to the curb."

"Okay." She disappeared and Adam reluctantly got into the chair. "We're going to miss you," she said as she pushed Adam out of his room. "You've been a terrific patient."

"The staff here has been wonderful," he replied. It was true. He'd had good treatment by doctors, nurses and all other staff.

Breanna was waiting for him at the curb and she hurried out of the driver's seat as they appeared. "You don't have to treat me like an invalid," he protested as she opened the car door for him.

He threw his duffel bag into the back seat, then got into the car. He was irritated and he didn't know why. He drew a deep breath to gain control as she got into the car and they pulled away from the curb.

"I'm leaving today." The words fell out of his mouth without his volition.

"I'm sure it will be good to be out of the hospital," she replied.

He realized she'd misunderstood what he was saying. "No, I mean I'm leaving Cherokee Corners. It's time for me to go home."

She took her foot off the gas and flashed him an unreadable look. "Are you sure? I mean, are you sure you're up to it?"

"I'm fine." He realized the thought of leaving was what was making him irritable. But he had to leave. All loose ends had been tidied up. Maggie was safe, Breanna was fine and Edward and Anita were thrilled by Maggie's existence and had already planned a trip to meet Maggie and Breanna next week.

"Where's Maggie?" he asked.

"Spending the night with my folks," she replied.

"How's she doing?"

"All right...considering." She tucked a strand of her long, dark shiny hair behind her ear. "Thank goodness Eddie wasn't mean to her. She only had nightmares for the first two nights. She's going to be just fine.''

''I'm glad.'' He stared out the passenger window and was grateful when she didn't say anything else. Telling her goodbye would be the most difficult thing he'd ever done, but he'd never been in the market for a long-standing relationship.

She parked in his driveway and together they got out of the car. ''Can I come in for a minute?'' she asked and gestured toward his cottage. ''I have something I want to talk to you about before you leave.''

He gazed at her curiously, but her expression gave nothing away. ''Sure, come on in.'' It seemed that in the past two weeks of his hospitalization they'd talked about everything under the sun. He couldn't imagine what she might possibly have to talk to him about before he left.

He dropped his duffel bag on the sofa, then turned to look at her. Goodbye would have been easier if she didn't look so beautiful, he thought. But clad in a sundress of rainbow colors, her skin looked like rich polished wood and her loose dark hair beckoned him to touch it…stroke the shiny length.

''What did you want to talk to me about?'' he asked.

She took a step closer to him and he tensed as her familiar, evocative scent surrounded him. ''Adam… don't go.''

Her simple words hit him like a blow in the gut. He suddenly recognized that the look radiating from her eyes was one of love. ''Breanna…don't.''

''Don't what? Don't tell you that I love you? Don't tell you that the thought of you going leaves a hollowness inside me?'' She stepped so close to him he could feel her body heat radiating to him. ''I swore to myself when Kurt left me that I'd never fall in love again, that I'd never share my life, my love with another man. But you changed that, Adam.''

''Breanna…'' He took a step back from her, desperately needing the distance. ''You're grateful to me, that's what it is. We shared a trauma with Maggie's kidnapping and that has you thinking you feel something that you don't.''

''Why would you believe that?'' she asked incredulously. ''Why would you believe that I don't love you?''

He raked a hand through his hair in frustration. ''Because you loved my cousin,'' he replied. ''Because you fell in love with Kurt and I am not like him, will never be anything like him. He was fun and adventurous, he exuded magnetism and a wildness that isn't in me.''

She stared at him for a long moment. ''Let me tell you something, Adam Spencer. When I met Kurt, he was pretending to be something he wasn't. He told me he was a bookkeeper on vacation. He led me to believe he was steady and responsible, caring and giving. I fell in love with the man he was pretending to be…and he was pretending to be you.''

He looked at her in astonishment.

''It's true,'' she said softly, stepping up before him once again. ''He made himself out to be a man just like you, Adam. A man who could be trusted, a man who would make me proud of who I am, a man that I could love with all my heart.''

She leaned forward and he couldn't help himself, he had to kiss her. He took possession of her mouth at the same time his arms wrapped around her. He knew kissing her was a mistake, that it would only make things more difficult, but he couldn't resist having one last taste of her mouth, one final embrace to last him a lifetime.

When the kiss ended, he moved away from her. "Breanna, you know it was never my intention to hurt you. But you also know it was never my intention to share a life with you. I told you from the very beginning that I didn't want a wife or children."

"But you love Maggie," she said softly, then raised her chin. "And you love me. I know you do, Adam. You can't deny it."

He didn't try to deny it. He did love her...loved her as he'd never loved before...as he'd probably never love again. "That doesn't change the fact that I'm leaving."

"But why?" Tears suddenly appeared in her eyes and he looked away, not wanting his last memory of her to be one of her weeping.

"I have a life to get back to." It was the only reason he could give. All he knew deep inside his heart, deep inside his soul, was the need to escape...escape from her and the love she offered, escape from Maggie and the uncertainty of raising a child. He looked back at her. "I never made any promises, Bree."

Despite the tears sparkling in her eyes, she raised her chin and eyed him proudly. "I won't beg you to stay, Adam. I love you. Maggie loves you. We could have built something together, but you're more like your cousin than you think. He ran from responsibility. He turned his back on me and his unborn child.

I'm not sure why you're running or from what...but I hope it's worth what you're leaving behind.''

She didn't wait for his reply, but turned and left the cottage. He drew an unsteady breath, feeling as if his limbs were suddenly weighed down by the tonnage of the world.

He wasn't running away, he told himself. He was just going home. He'd taken care of Kurt's final mess and it was time to leave.

It took him only an hour to gather his things in his car. As he packed, he studiously kept his thoughts from Breanna and Maggie. Instead, he thought of all the things he needed to do when he got back to Kansas City.

Maybe it was time to move to the suburbs, get out of his high-rise and into a neighborhood. He could move to a little ranch where he'd have a yard to mow. Maybe he'd get a dog.

Neither Breanna nor Maggie were outside when he got in his car to leave. He stood for a moment and looked at their house, wondering if he wasn't making the mistake of his lifetime.

She loved him. She loved him and Maggie loved him. He got into his car and pulled out of the driveway. As he pointed the nose of the car toward the highway that would take him back to his life in Kansas City, he told her she was wrong, he wasn't anything like Kurt.

He didn't run from responsibility, he embraced it. He met life head-on, plowing through instead of racing to the next adventure.

He was nothing like Kurt...nothing. Then why are

you running away? a little voice whispered inside his head. What are you running from? And what are you running to?

She watched from her front window as he pulled out of his driveway and disappeared from sight. Her heart was broken into a million pieces, and she knew it would be a very long time before the pieces found their way back together again.

She'd had hope. Each day as she'd sat in the hospital room with him and they'd talked, she'd believed there was a chance for them.

Those hours with him had merely drawn her closer to him than she'd already been. She couldn't deny the fact that she was grateful to him. He had saved her life. The bullet Eddie Duncan had fired from his gun had been intended for her and Adam had thrown his own body in the way to save her.

But, gratitude aside, she was deeply in love with him. And now he was gone. She was glad she had the house to herself. Maggie was at her parents' place and Rachel was on an outing with David, leaving her to deal with her grief all alone.

She hadn't wanted to fall in love, had thought she was perfectly satisfied living her life alone with just her family and Maggie to fill in the empty spots. But there had been an emptiness inside her that no family or daughter could fill. Adam had filled it.

She moved through the lower level of the house like a zombie, willing herself not to spill any tears, reminding herself that he'd been honest about the fact that he didn't want a wife or a family from the very beginning.

She couldn't even be angry with him. It wasn't his fault she'd fallen in love with him. She'd survived the kidnapping of her daughter. She would survive this pain as well.

Cleaning. That's what she needed to do. She'd clean the house from top to bottom and maybe in the process exhaust herself so that she didn't have the energy to think about Adam and all that would never be.

Cleaning didn't help. Twenty minutes later she was upstairs in her room dusting the dresser with tears streaking down her cheeks.

Somehow Adam had made her believe again in the dreams she'd once entertained. He'd made her think about a happy marriage with a strong, committed man. He'd reminded her of dreams of working together, building a future, sleeping in somebody's arms.

Adam, her heart cried. Adam, I love you.

She jumped up off the bed as she heard the front door crash open. For a split second an irrational fear swept through her. Eddie! He's come to finish the job!

"Breanna!"

It wasn't Eddie's voice that called her name. It was Adam's. What was he doing back here? "I'm up here," she called and quickly swiped at her tears. She didn't want him to see her crying.

She heard him coming, taking the stairs two at a time and when he entered her bedroom he filled it with a barely suppressed energy. "We need to talk," he said.

"Talk?" She stared at him blankly, wondering what had brought him back here. What more they could possibly have to say to one another.

"I got twenty miles down the highway and realized you'd once asked me a question that I'd never answered, and it was suddenly important that I answer it.''

She sat on the edge of the bed, looking at him in confusion. He remained just inside the doorway returning her gaze with intensity. "What question?" she asked.

He raked a hand through his hair and broke eye contact. Instead he stared at someplace just over her head. "You asked me once what it was I got out of my relationship with Kurt. What kept me taking care of his life and cleaning up his messes. At the time you asked, I didn't have an answer and it bothered me. I knew it was important that I discover the answer, but I didn't seem to be able to come up with one.''

"And you have now?"

Once again he looked at her, his eyes so blue they made her ache inside. "I have my answer. As long as I had Kurt's life to deal with, I didn't have to have a life of my own." He took a step toward her, his brow drawn into a deep furrow. "It's so much easier, so much more self-protective to deal with somebody else's life. There's no emotional involvement, little chance for pain.''

"And little chance for any real joy or happiness," she replied.

"You're right. You are so right." He walked over to where she sat, took her hand and pulled her to her feet. "I had decided I didn't want any children because I'd watched my aunt and uncle be hurt over and over again by Kurt. I didn't want anyone to have that kind of power over me.''

Despite the fact that he was holding her hands, that he gazed deeply into her eyes, she was afraid to hope.

"There are no guarantees with children, Adam. You can love them, but they can get sick or bad things can happen to them, or they can make bad choices. But heartache isn't all there is to parenthood. You haven't considered the joy."

"I've experienced the joy...with Maggie." He smiled, a beautiful smile that seemed to light him from within. The smile faltered a bit. "And I've experienced the pain and fear of the possibility of losing her."

"But Adam, there is more joy than pain...and not every child is like Kurt was."

"I know. Maggie fills my heart." He dropped her hands and instead placed his hands on either side of her face. "And you fill my heart. Bree, I don't want to go back to my life in Kansas City. It wasn't a life at all. You make me feel alive. You make me feel as if there is no end to the possibilities for happiness. You were a loose end that wrapped around my heart and made me captive. I love you, Bree."

"Oh, Adam." Tears of joy splashed her cheeks and then he was kissing her...a kiss filled with passion, a kiss filled with sweet love.

"Marry me, Bree," he said as the kiss ended. "I can't think of any other family I'd rather be a part of, I can't think of any other little girl I'd rather be a father to and I can't think of any other woman I'd rather share my life with than you."

"Yes," she exclaimed, laughing and crying at the same time. "Oh, yes, I'll marry you." As he pulled her closer against him and once again claimed her lips with his, the craziest thought went through her mind.

She remembered the alert that had trailed at the bottom of the television screen when Maggie had been missing and in her mind a new alert was playing. Breanna James…last seen in the arms of love…last seen in Adam's arms.

Alyssa Whitefeather had just served a double dip of Rocky Road ice cream when the headache pierced through her left eye, a warning that a vision was imminent. "Sarah, take over for me, would you?"

With the pain nearly blinding, Alyssa left the ice-cream parlor and went into the living area in the back. She stumbled to the sofa and sat down.

Blackness…waves of it consumed her. And with the darkness came the horror, a yawning greedy beast of horror that swept over her, through her. And with the horror came the certainty that evil approached and threatened somebody she loved. It was an evil so dark, so malevolent it terrified her.

She awakened fifteen minutes later to find herself lying on the sofa. Slowly, she pulled herself up to a sitting position, her heart racing with fear.

When Maggie had been kidnapped, Alyssa had thought that's what the visions had portended. But Maggie was safe and sound and the horrible darkness still haunted Alyssa. This was the third time she'd suffered the awful blackness since Maggie had been recovered safe and sound.

Something was going to happen…something bad, and until the visions revealed something more than darkness and terror, there was nothing Alyssa could do to stop it. All she could do was wait for it to happen.

Epilogue

The darkness filled the bedroom, broken by streams of moonlight that danced into the window and across the bed. Adam loved the way his wife looked when she was bathed in moonlight. He loved the way his wife looked in any light.

They had married a week ago in a small ceremony at city hall. Adam had never known how rich life could be until now. He awakened in the mornings to Maggie kisses and sunshine, to challenges of opening a new office and Breanna's love and support.

She raised her head and smiled at him, her eyes shining in the glow of the moonlight. "What are you thinking, Mr. Spencer?"

He returned her smile and stroked a hand down her silky bare back. "I'm just lying here thinking about what a lucky man I am, Mrs. Spencer."

"That's funny, I was just lying here thinking about what a lucky woman I am."

"You know this is a forever kind of thing," he said to her.

"I wouldn't have it any other way," she replied. She cuddled closer to him and sighed with obvious contentment. "I've never been so happy in my life, Adam."

"I feel the same way. I never knew what it felt like to have a full heart, but you fill my heart, sweet Bree." They both jumped in surprise as the telephone rang.

"It's after eleven, who could that be?" she murmured as she reached over to answer. "Hello? Hi, Clay." A frown worried itself across her forehead and she sat up. Adam sat up as well and turned on the light on the nightstand.

"What's going on? Yes...yes...we're on our way." She hung up the phone and looked at him. "That was Clay. He said we need to get out to my parents' place right away."

"Did he say why?" Adam got out of bed and pulled on a pair of jeans.

She stood and reached for the clothes she'd thrown on a chair before bedtime. "He wouldn't say. He said we just need to get out there." She looked at him, fear darkening her eyes. "There was something in Clay's voice...something that frightened me."

Adam walked around the bed and pulled her into his arms. "There's nothing to be afraid of," he said. "Whatever is going on we'll face it together."

She smiled up at him. "Together. I love the way that sounds. I love you, Adam."

"And I love you, Bree." He claimed her lips in a kiss that spoke of his devotion, his desire, his love for her. "And whatever we face in the future, we face together."

"And we'll be fine because we have the strength of our love to support us," she replied.

As he hugged her once again, he silently thanked his cousin. Kurt hadn't left him one final loose end, rather he'd pointed him to a path that had led to a future filled with joy and love...a future filled with Maggie and Breanna.

*   *   *   *   *

*Watch for the second installment
in the* CHEROKEE CORNERS *series,*

DEAD CERTAIN,

*coming in October 2003
from Silhouette Intimate Moments*

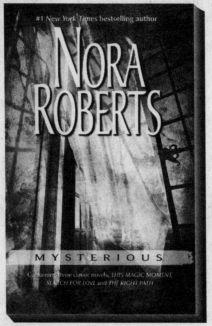

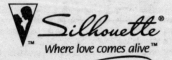

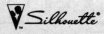

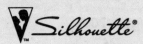

COMING NEXT MONTH

SIMCNM0703